WHEN A GANGSTA FALLS IN *Love* 3

A NOVEL BY

ROBIN

PROLOGUE

On some other shit...

Baby Girl walked into her bathroom, dying to soak her body in the tub. She had just done a ten hour shift at the strip club, and all she wanted to do was relax. She was also excited about the new waterproof toys she had just gotten in the mail as well. Baby Girl hadn't been getting any dick since she had stopped prostituting and fucking on Oxy. She decided to retire her pussy and learn how to pleasure herself. She had fallen in love with clit stimulation, so she bought every vibrator she knew would have her reaching her peak.

Baby Girl slipped out of her robe, grabbing her glass of wine and new vibrator. She sipped her wine while she found a nice video on PornHub. After finding one of her favorite lesbian videos, she propped her tablet on the stand on the counter, and then she downed her wine. The warmness from the wine had her clit tingling. She stepped into the hot bubbly water and sat down. She laid back and turned on her vibrator. She put her hand under the water and started massaging her clit.

"Mmmm."

She let out a light moan as she watched the two girls on her tablet suck on each other's breasts. She turned up the speed. She didn't know why she was so turned on by women lately, but it almost had her thinking she should find herself a girlfriend.

Baby Girl rubbed her vibrator around her clit and up and down her vulva. It felt amazing to be pleasing herself and not some man. She was finally in tune with her body and knew how it felt to be pleased and not be the pleaser.

She opened her legs wider and slid her vibrator in and out of her hole. That's when she felt herself about to come. Baby Girl let out a loud sexy moan. She lived alone, so she could make as much noise as she wanted. She pinched one of her nipples and started rubbing her vibrator on her clit again. Within seconds, she was coming in her bath water. She closed her eyes to catch her breath and dropped her vibrator on the floor. At that moment, she opened her eyes, because a loud smell of weed smoke hit her nose, and she hadn't even lit her blunt yet. When she turned around, she thought she had seen a ghost. Oxy was standing in the doorway of her bathroom with a blunt in between his lips. He took his blunt from his mouth and smirked.

"Pussy ain't had no attention in a long time, huh?" Oxy said as he walked over to the tub.

"Nigga, what the fuck are you doing in my house, and how the fuck did you get in here?" Baby Girl shouted as she jumped out of the tub and wrapped her robe around herself. She didn't know how long he was standing there watching her. She was shook and embarrassed.

"I picked your cheap ass lock with a credit card," he smirked. He knew Baby Girl was going to be pissed off, but she was his only option.

"Well, what the fuck do you want, Oxy? You are messing up my relaxation time."

Baby Girl was irritated to the core that he had broken into her house. If he wasn't him, she would have called the police.

"I need Amiah's new number. She broke up with me a week ago, and I need to tell her something important."

"Broke up?"

She shook her head.

"Well, can you wait your ass in the living room until I get dressed? Damn, you are buggin' right now!"

He walked out of the bathroom and headed to the living room. He didn't care about Baby Girl's chill time. He needed Amiah's number, because her old number was disconnected. Baby Girl rushed into her room, closed the door, and locked it, making sure Oxy didn't walk into her room. She had no kind of feelings for him anymore, so barging into her room would really be unacceptable. She threw on a pair of pajama pants and a sports bra. She slapped on some lotion and untied her hair. She then walked out of the room and went into the kitchen for another drink, but Oxy had beat her to the punch. When she walked in, Oxy was opening her fresh bottle of Hennessy that she had left on her counter.

"Oxy, you can't just be breaking into my crib. Now, I have to change my locks."

Baby Girl grabbed two shot glasses from the cabinet. She grabbed the bottle from Oxy's hand and poured herself a shot.

"Look, I just came here to get Miah's number. She broke up with me, and I need to talk to her."

He picked up the Hennessy bottle and drank his shot from the bottle. Baby Girl looked at him and could tell he was stressed out. He had grown a shadow beard, and he was wearing a pair of sweats, a t-shirt, and a snapback that said No Brakes, Los Angeles. She had never seen Oxy without a haircut and a shave, so she knew this was big, but she wasn't sure about giving him Amiah's number. She didn't even know what was going on with the two of them.

"Well, since she changed her number because y'all broke up, I don't think I should give it to you. She told me she got a new number because she got a new phone. She didn't mention anything about a breakup."

"Look, Baby Girl, I am not leaving until you give me that number. I'll camp out on your couch until you give it to me."

Oxy walked into the living room with Baby Girl's Hennessy bottle and flopped on her white leather couch. He started taking off his Nikes and reached for her Firestick remote. Oxy looked serious about staying, and Baby Girl did not want him on her couch, funking it up. She knew Oxy was a clean dude, but she didn't let anyone sleep on her couch… not even herself, because it was white. Baby Girl walked over to her island and dug into her purse. She pulled out her phone and tossed it to him.

"Get the number and go, Oxy. You are putting me in a position I don't want to be in, and that's fucked up."

She was overly annoyed with his presence and hated the fact that he was putting her in his and Amiah's mix when she didn't know what happened. If giving him the number would get him out of her house, he could have it.

He texted the number to his phone and stood up.

"Good looking out, Baby Girl. I'm glad to see you and Amiah are good friends now… thanks to me and all. That's a good look for you."

He opened the front door and left, leaving her phone on the couch. Baby Girl took a deep breath and sat on her barstool. She contemplated calling Amiah but decided not to. It was a Tuesday, and she knew Amiah was somewhere studying. Amiah had made it a rule that she didn't take any calls on Tuesday nights so that she could get her work done and attend her evening class. She was due to see Amiah the next day, so she decided to wait and tell her face to face. Baby Girl decided to call Bayley and warn her about Oxy, just in case he started bugging her to get in contact with Miah.

Baby Girl locked her door and put a chair under the nob. She was now nervous and couldn't change her locks until the next day. She grabbed her Hennessey and blunt, heading to her room to call Bayley and continue enjoying her night.

Baby Girl dialed Bayley's number, and she answered on the first ring.

"What's up, Reeka?" Bayley said, sounding like she was sleeping.

"My bad if I woke you up, but this nigga, Oxy, broke into my house and demanded Amiah's new number. I don't know what's going on with them, but he said they broke up."

Baby Girl lit her blunt and shook her head.

"Wow, are you fucking serious? So… what else did he say? I wonder why she ain't told us."

Baby Girl shook her head and blew smoke from her nose.

"Girl, I don't even know… and his ass looks stressed to. He came up in here being a bully. I've never seen him like this, but I am going to let you go back to sleep. I guess we can talk to her tomorrow at her photoshoot. You know how she is about Tuesdays."

"Damn. Well, I am going to shoot her a text and just ask how she is doing. I won't mention the breakup until she answers back. If she doesn't, I'll wait. I knew something was up with her. She's been distant since she said she had gotten sick before she picked me up from jail. Just call me in the morning when you are on your way."

Baby Girl agreed and hung up the phone. She couldn't believe Oxy and Amiah were broken up, and she couldn't wait to find out what had happened.

***

Oxy sat behind the wheel of his black 2015 rented Ferrari and dialed Amiah's number five times. After realizing she wasn't going to answer, he decided to block his number. The phone rang a few times, and Amiah finally answered.

"What do you want, Oxy? I know this is you," Amiah said in an agitated tone. She knew it was him calling from a blocked number.

"So… I am Oxy now, huh?" he asked. He had gotten used to

her calling him Brandon and not Oxy. That was what separated their relationship from his street life.

"Yes, because you belong to the streets, and that's what they call you. Don't your bitches call you that?"

"Damn, will you quit with the smart shit? I want you to talk to me, Miah. Look, I'm sorry you had to find out the way you did, but I never meant to hurt you. I swear. I love you, babe," he pleaded.

"Well, it happened. I found it, and this is done. I will not tolerate you cheating on me. You really have lost your fucking mind."

"Can you just meet me at my house so that we can talk… please?"

He was hoping for a yes, but Amiah was not budging.

"Look, I have to go. I am on my way inside my evening class, so I don't have time to meet you. Please stop calling my phone. Bye."

She hung up before he could say anything. When he tried to call her back, her phone went to voicemail on the first ring. She had turned off her phone.

"Fuck!"

Oxy punched his steering wheel. He was already tired of Amiah dissing him, and it had only been a few days. He was madder at himself than he was with Amiah not agreeing to talk to him, though. He knew it was all his fault, and it was nothing he could do about it. Fucking with Erica was one of his many mistakes he wished he never did. He had hurt Amiah and never wanted her to find out. Now, he was feeling like a hopeless lame for messing around on the woman he loved.

Oxy started up the car and drove off. He decided he would head to his studio and join the party that was going on there. A local rapper had paid him $10,000 to rent the studio for two days and shoot a video. He knew once he surrounded himself with liquor and girls, he would get Amiah off his mind for a very short while. When he walked in, women and dudes were sitting everywhere while a cameraman walked around filming. Oxy spotted Meeze, BR, and BR's girlfriend sitting on one of the couches. Meeze was popping a bottle of D'USSÉ while BR talked to his girl and rolled a blunt.

"Ayyyyee, my nigga is here. What's up, bro?" Meeze said with a big cheesy smile. He knew what Oxy was going through, so he acknowledged him with much love every time he saw him to lift his spirits. The two of them slapped fives, and Oxy flopped on the couch.

"What's up, my niggas? I see I'm just in time," Oxy said as he picked up a cup from the table, so that he could take a shot of D'USSÉ.

"Yup!"

Meeze filled Oxy's small Styrofoam cup halfway.

"Aye, where Bay at? I need to talk to her," Oxy asked Meeze. Meeze laughed.

"She's at the house, big pregnant and shit. She ain't fuckin' with a nigga right now since that jail shit. She doesn't want to go anywhere with me," Meeze said, downing his shot of liquor.

"Why, what's up?"

"I need her to get in Miah's ear for me."

Meeze laughed.

"She's not fucking with you, bro. I don't think she knows,

8

because she ain't said shit, but if I tell her that, she is going to flip. In the meantime, lil' mama over there that keeps eyeing you been asking about you all night. She looks like your type. Holla at her," Meeze expressed. He wanted his boy to cheer up. Oxy sipped his liquor.

"Yeah... I hear you, bro."

As the party went on, Oxy started mingling around the room and ended up talking to the girl that kept eyeing him all night. He thought she was cute, and she favored Amiah a lot, but her ass was a little fatter. Oxy gazed into the girl's eyes with his red glossy eyes. He was trying to figure out who she really was. He could have sworn she was Amiah, for sure.

"So, Amiah, how old are you again?" Oxy asked in a drunken slur. The girl giggled and wrapped her arms around his neck. From the moment Oxy walked in, she was ready to be under him. She knew he had a girlfriend, because she saw a picture of him and Amiah on his Instagram page. She had come across his face in her feed a couple of months prior and stalked his page ever since. She was hoping to go home with him, even though he was calling her a different name.

"I told you... my name is not Amiah. It's Elecia, and I am twenty-two. Do you own this place, or is that a rumor?" she smiled. She was a little drunk as well and felt like she had him right where she wanted.

"My bad, Elecia. You look like this girl I used to know... but yeah, this is all mine, so are you riding with a nigga tonight or what? I'm ready to get out of here," he grabbed her ass and pulled her close. Feeling his touch turned her on.

"If that's what you want, then yeah. I'll leave with you. I just have to let my friend know."

When the girl walked off to talk to her friend, Meeze and BR walked up to him. Oxy was staggering drunk. He kept his cool, but BR and Meeze were his boys, so they knew he was over his limit. He had his snapback brim low over his eyes, and he was leaning against the wall with a smirk on his face.

"Bro, I know you came in that rented joint and don't want to crash that shit. I'll drive you back, and you can pick your shit up in the morning," Meeze said.

"Yeah. You fucked up, my boy. I'll follow y'all out there since I've sobered up," BR said in his accent.

"Nah, I'm good. I'mma have Amiah with me, so I'm good."

Oxy smirked. Meeze shook his head.

"Bro, that's not Amiah. Just give me the keys, and I'll take y'all to your crib," Meeze insisted.

"Nah, a nigga ain't that drunk to leave the whip parked here. Just give me some water, and I'm good."

BR shrugged.

"We can't let the boy drive to Calabasas by himself. We gotta follow him, at least."

"I agree. He's called that girl, Amiah, all night, and personally, I don't trust her," BR's girlfriend added.

"So, you sure you want to bring her to the crib?" Meeze asked.

"Yup... I want her," Oxy said, long and drawn out. After Oxy grabbed a couple of waters, they all headed to the parking lot. When he and Elecia got into his car, he downed his water and then let the top down. It was a little cold, but he knew the cool breeze would keep him awake on his forty-five-minute drive.

He hooked his phone to the Bluetooth of the car, and Young Dolph's song, "Preach It," started blaring through his luxury speakers. He was glad that the song started playing, because that was his mood. He was cold, bitter, and had done a lot of thinking.

Keep it real with your dawg no matter what, (Preach).

Same bitch that claim she love you she'll set you up, (Preach).

Out here in these streets, it ain't no such thing as love, (Preach).

The only thing I trust is this pistol and these slugs, (Preach).

Real nigga shit, only what I do and speak. If he don't work at all, he a fuckin' leech, (Preach).

I ain't got shit for a nigga, ain't nothing in this mothafuckin' world free, (Preach).

"Are you scared?" he asked with a smirk as he backed out his parking space. She smiled.

"Why should I be?"

"Because my last girl told me that I ain't shit, and I drive fast."

Oxy was talking crazy since he was drunk. After his breakup, he definitely was starting to feel like an ain't shit nigga. Every time he thought about the fact that he gave in to Erica, made him so angry. Erica was definitely poison, and he wished he never hired her. Elecia laughed.

"Ain't shit, huh? Well, I only want you for tonight, so you *not being shit* don't faze me. Hell, I ain't shit either," she sat back and put on her seatbelt. At that moment, Oxy realized she was not Amiah. She was just some broad trying to get his money and some dick. He knew Amiah would never leave the studio with some stranger. She had class and had respect for herself. Therefore, he was just going to use her for what she was for the night and take her back to where she belonged the next morning. Oxy drove off slowly down the alleyway, but once he hit the freeway, he grabbed his half of blunt from the ashtray, turned up his music, and started doing ninety on the freeway with Meeze and BR trailing behind him as much as they could.

When they got to his house, all of them had more drinks and a couple more blunts. Then, Oxy and Elecia headed to his room. He was officially over this limit and was having a change of heart about his company he brought home. He just wanted to go to sleep, because he knew he had a lot of work to do later that day. It was already three in the morning. He sat at the edge of his bed and slid his royal blue Nike Cortez off. Then, he took off his shirt, leaving on his tank top.

"Your house is really nice. You live here alone?" Elecia asked as she looked out his balcony at the water. The waves were crashing, giving her a good view along with the full moon shining over the water.

"Yup," he said in a nonchalant tone. He stood up and walked to his walk-in closet to slip out his jeans.

"You are really living it up. I might have to keep you longer than one night," she smirked. She was really feeling his swag. Seeing that he really lived the life he showed on his page really made her have a change of heart about just having him one night. Oxy walked out his closet wearing a pair of gray sweats.

"I doubt that."

She was not moving in on his space, and he didn't even want to give her a hint that she could. The only woman he wanted to move in was Amiah. Elecia walked over to him and wrapped her arms around his waist.

"Well, let's not get wrapped up in what I want. I want to know what I can do for you tonight."

She looked up at him and smiled.

"How about you go take a shower, and we can talk about that when you get out."

Elecia unwrapped her arms from his waist and headed for his master bathroom in his room. While she was in the bathroom, Oxy started to get dizzy from all the drink in his system. He laid across his bed and threw his arm over his face. He started to slowly drift off to sleep until Elecia came back into the room.

"Wake up, sleepy head," Elecia said, standing on the side of the bed. When he opened his left eye, she was standing there with her hair pulled up in a bun and a black towel wrapped around her. He smirked. He knew she was ready to play, but he was ready to sleep.

"A nigga tired than a mothafucka now, since you took so long in the shower."

She giggled.

"I was only in there fifteen minutes, silly."

Elecia sat next to him on the bed and started rubbing on his dick print through his sweats. He wasn't even hard yet, and he had to already be at least eight inches. She slowly started to feel his dick rise, and it excited her, so she reached her hand inside his sweats and Hanes boxer briefs.

"So, you brought me here to sleep… or to have fun?" Elecia asked as she pulled his dick out and started stroking it. Oxy was so sleepy that he was just telling her anything.

"I brought you here to do whatever you want to do, lil' mama."

She smiled.

"Well, you continue to lay back, and let me do my thing."

After that, no words were spoken. Elecia took all of him into her mouth and started sucking him slowly. Oxy let out a light grunt at the feeling of her tongue. He closed his eyes and tried to enjoy it for as long as he could. However, after ten minutes of pleasure, he was snoring. Elecia tried to keep him hard, but once he fell into a deep sleep, his dick went all the way limp. She was so disappointed. She was far away from where she lived. She couldn't do what she wanted to do to him, and had no ride home. Therefore, she crawled under the sheet and fell asleep, feeling played and disappointed on her mission to get Oxy...

***

Oxy walked out of his master bathroom with a bottle of 800mg Ibuprofen in his hand. His head was pounding, and he couldn't stop throwing up liquor. His stomach felt like somebody was ripping his insides out. It was now five days into his breakup with Amiah. All he had been doing was drinking, partying in the studio, and trying to bury himself in work. Now, it was finally catching up to him. His shoe company was taking off fast, and he had nobody doing paperwork for him, so he had to do as much as he could by himself to keep his mind off his problems.

After Amiah told him to leave her alone, that only made him want to pursue her more. Therefore, he was going to be paying her a visit soon. He knew he had fucked up, but he felt like things could be fixed. He hadn't heard anything from Erica, and the police were constantly coming to the studio, leaving business cards for someone to come forward on what happened, but Oxy was refusing to talk. He was going to handle Coby on his own, because he knew for a fact it was him.

Oxy staggered into his bedroom. He wanted to lay down and go back to sleep, but when he saw Elecia tangled up in his black sheets, he decided not to. He didn't even remember bringing her home with him. He looked at the alarm clock on his nightstand and saw that it was four in the afternoon. He never slept that late, so he headed downstairs to find some water and food so that he could take his pills.

When he finally made it down his spiral stairs, he heard men laughing and smelled food cooking. He immediately knew who the voices belonged to. It was BR and Meeze. They were in his den, playing on the PlayStation. He decided to walk into the kitchen first. He spotted BR's longtime girlfriend whipping up some fried chicken, greens, mac and cheese, and beef patties. His stomach rumbled when he glanced at the chicken frying away on his huge stove.

"What's up, Leah? How y'all niggas get in my house?" Oxy said, sounding groggy while trying to reach for a piece of chicken. Leah laughed and popped his hand away from her chicken.

"Don't come in here touching my chicken. Your ass was fucked up last night, so we followed you home to make sure you were okay. You insisted that you bring that girl home with you that's in your bed, and your drunk ass kept calling her Amiah. You need to get your life, boy… for real."

Leah passed him a chicken wing and then laughed.

"Damn," was all Oxy could say. He didn't hesitate to take the piece of chicken. He bit down into it and then walked over to his refrigerator to grab a bottle of water. He opened his bottle of pills and took two, even though he was supposed to only take one. He was feeling that bad. When he walked into the den, Meeze looked up at Oxy and laughed.

"Bro, what's the deal? Niggas have been waiting up for you since ten this morning. You were fucked up last night," Meeze expressed loudly.

"Yeah, I know. Leah told me. What y'all niggas got going today, though… besides funkin' up my crib with chicken and weed?"

Oxy laid back on his love seat and closed his eyes.

"Shit, niggas were just making sure you weren't dead up there with that bitch. You can't live like this, bro. You drink, but you don't drink like how you been doing, so me and BR got a plan."

Meeze rubbed his hands together. He was excited about their next move.

"You need to go get you a passport, because we're taking a vacation from this place. You need to get you some real pussy from a Jamaican gal with a fat ass. Bitch will suck your dick so good… you are going to want to bring her back to the States with you and marry her," BR said in his thick Jamaican accent. Oxy chuckled. BR had been trying to get him to go to Jamaica for the longest just to see how they live. However, with the hectic life Oxy was living and with Pricey living in his home at the time he first asked, he knew there was no way he could leave his property alone in the states while he was on vacation. Now, he felt like it was much needed. He had been working hard and dealing with a lot of drama, so he was definitely with taking a trip to Jamaica.

"Shit, that's what's up. I'm with it."

As they sat there talking about their upcoming trip, Elecia came into the den. She was smiling and wearing her clothes from the night before. She walked over to Oxy and sat next to him. The moment was so awkward, but nobody said a word. They both were used to Oxy being with Amiah, and not Elecia.

"Sooo, how am I getting home?" Elecia said in an aggravated tone, noticing the awkward silence.

"You should have thought about that before you came to some strange nigga's crib. Your mama never taught you about stranger danger?" Meeze shot at her. Elecia smacked her lips.

"Whatever, I don't have time for childish niggas. I was just trying to see how I was getting home. I'll just take an Uber. I'll see you around, Oxy."

She stormed out the den without letting Oxy say a word. He would have at least taken her to the city later that night, but since she had an attitude, he let her go. BR and Meeze busted out in laughter.

17

"Bro... I fell asleep on her last night, so she is hot," Oxy said.

"Damn, so y'all ain't do shit?" Meeze asked in a shocked tone.

"Nah. A nigga fell asleep. The last thing I remembered is her suckin' my dick."

BR and Meeze laughed.

"You tapped out on the pussy. You definitely need a vacation," BR said.

"Man, don't ever let me go out like that again. I'm cool on these bitches. They are nothing but thirst traps. After that Erica shit, I'm good," Oxy expressed. After Amiah left him, he honestly didn't want anybody. His emotions and liquor had him acting out, and he knew he needed to change, especially if he wanted Amiah back.

After they clowned on Elecia for a while, they finally got up and headed for the kitchen to eat. After Oxy devoured his late lunch, he was feeling so much better. He decided to head to his office and do some work while his boys booked their trip in the den. As Oxy went over all his numbers, he realized his savings account was almost at a million. Although he was making big purchases, he was still generating legit money. He had accounts with millionaires that were making purchases five times a day. Now, Oxy was really looking forward to his vacation as a celebration for his success, but he wished he had his lady to share it with him.

CHAPTER ONE

Weary...

But you know that a King is only a man.

With flesh and bones, he bleeds just like you do.

He said, "Where does that leave you?

And do you belong?"

I do. - Solange.

*A*miah stood in front of the white backdrop in a private photo studio in Hollywood, posing for pictures for her promotional cover of her mixtape called, "All I Have," while Solange's "*Seat at the Table*" album played throughout the studio. She was wearing a pair of stone washed skinny jeans, a white shirt that read *My Black is Bomb,* and she had a colorful African headwrap on her hair with her now blonde bangs flowing out the front. She was wearing a pair of orange heels to match the orange in her head wrap.

"That's right, Miss Miah. Work it," the cameraman said as he took flick after flick, trying to catch the right shot. For this to be her first photoshoot, she thought she was doing a great job.

Amiah was so excited about getting her mixtape on DatPiff, and she knew girls would love the way she was promoting black women with her attire for the cover art. Although she and Oxy were broken up, she wasn't going to sit around and be depressed about it. She was still going to continue her music career and finish school. Oxy had played a big part in her music career, but after she did some research, she found herself a new manager and studio to record in. Anything with Oxy's name on it, she wanted nothing to do with. She wanted to push him far in the back of her brain and just move on.

She was finally ready to break the news to Baby Girl and Bayley. She knew they were going to be shocked and disappointed, but she was doing what was best for her and not the people around her.

Amiah looked over at the door and smiled when she saw Bayley and Baby Girl walk in together. Just a couple of months ago, they were enemies. Now, they were close as ever. Bayley was almost five months pregnant and already looking like she was ready to have the baby. After Amiah bailed her out of jail, Meeze vowed to Amiah and Bayley that he wouldn't put her in any more danger. He was going to do his business on his own and let Bayley enjoy her pregnancy like she wanted to. Amiah told the cameraman that she was going to take a quick break to talk to her best friends.

"Dang, best friend. This is fly, and you looking real cute!" Bayley said when she walked up to Amiah.

"Yeah, girl. You are looking real *afrodesiac-ish* and shit!" Baby Girl said in an excited tone.

"Thank you. Y'all are also looking real cute too… as always. I want y'all to take some pictures with me before we leave," Amiah said as she hugged them both. The three of them walked over by a window where there were some chairs and a table. The sun was shining brightly through the window. It was a beautiful spring day. When they sat down, Bayley and Baby Girl's smiles immediately turned into sad faces while Amiah continued to smile at them.

"What's up with y'all? Why y'all looking like sad dogs all of a sudden?" Amiah asked in a confused tone.

"Are you okay? Why you didn't tell us you and Oxy broke up?" Bayley asked in a sincere tone. Amiah's smile turned into a sad face like theirs.

"How did you guys find out?" Amiah said in a low child-like tone as she fiddled with her nails. Every time she thought about herself and Oxy, it made her sad, but she knew she couldn't drown in misery thinking about him. Although she was going to tell them anyway, she was still shocked that they knew.

"He broke into Baby Girl's house to get your number, and he told her," Bayley said. Amiah shook her head.

"He is so crazy and acting out like a fool right now."

"Miah, he broke in and claimed he wasn't leaving 'til he got it. I just wanted him to go. I knew once he called you, you would block him, so I just gave it to him."

"Don't worry about it. He's going to be a pest to all of us until I take him back, and I don't plan on doing that."

"So, damn… what the fuck happened?" Baby Girl asked. She and

Bayley were all ears.

"I caught him cheating with his receptionist. She was sucking him up..."

Baby Girl and Bayley both gasped.

"I'm so sorry, best friend!"

Bayley stood up from her chair and hugged Amiah. They were so close that she could feel her pain. Baby Girl shook her head. Out of all the niggas she encountered, she thought for sure Oxy wasn't a cheater, but he had proved her wrong. As soon as Bayley's arms wrapped around Amiah, tears started flooding her face, smearing her mascara.

"He went through all of that to get me, and turns around and does what he promised he would never do, and that was betray me. I trusted him with everything. He was there with me when my mom died. He helped me get my music off the ground. Then, he just cheats on me. I just don't understand! All I told him was I wanted to take a break from sex and he blocked me out like I wasn't a priority anymore. That's why I suspected him of cheating. And he really was," she cried out, making Bayley and Baby Girl extremely upset. They were frowning and on the verge of tears just like her. They knew how much she loved Oxy, and he went and did her wrong for no reason.

"Damn, now I want to beat his ass. He is truly a fraud for cheating on you, best friend."

Bayley was disappointed in Oxy. She truly thought he was the one for her best friend.

"Yeah... that's fucked up, lil' mama. I am glad you are holding your head up, though. These niggas come a dime a dozen. They all have flaws, and they all have needs. Whatever you were lacking in, I bet that bitch was so called doing it. I've seen it all. Once you stop sucking that nigga's dick, the next bitch gonna have her lips wrapped around it. I've been on both sides, and honestly, they both suck. I never understood a cheating ass nigga."

Bayley nodded her head.

"That shit is so true. I really do believe the majority of men cheat, especially since this fool cheated. I can't believe him… ugh."

Amiah sat up straight. She reached for her purse and pulled out her mirror to fix her makeup.

"Well, I just want to move forward and continue my life. I'll be nineteen soon, and I am living on my own, now that my mom is gone. I have a lot of time to figure out what I want to do as far as relationships, but for now, he has to suffer. I was so embarrassed and hurt. That's why I didn't tell you guys. I was snooping and found a surveillance of them in his office at the studio. I was so mad. I broke his china cabinet with all his mom's crystal pieces and his coffee table. Then, I left before he got there. It was when we were supposed to go to Vegas for New Years, and I told y'all I had gotten sick."

"Damn, I need a drink after all of that. So, what have you been doing? I think you need to have some fun outside of school and work," Baby Girl said.

"Yeah, I've been wanting to go out and be around some sexy faces. I was thinking the strip club."

Bayley and Baby Girl laughed.

"Yeah, let's go to the strip club tonight. You need a break," Bayley added. She was pregnant, but she would do anything to see Amiah happy again. After the girls talked a little more, they headed back to the photoshoot and took a bunch of pictures. Amiah felt a sense of relief after telling her friends it was over between her and Oxy. Now, with the support of them, she knew she could move forward with her life...

***

Two Weeks Later...

Baby Girl sat in Amiah's passenger seat, looking down at her $20,000 cashier's check she had just gotten from the bank. Baby Girl had finally gotten accepted into USC for journalism and a few other classes. Now all she needed to do was pay her tuition for the whole school year. She was ecstatic that she had saved money from stripping, not having to prostitute, and able to put it to good use. She was finally feeling like a woman and not some strip hoe. Amiah parked in the student parking lot, and the girls got out. They headed straight to the student center.

"Are you ready to do this, girl?" Amiah asked with a huge smile on her face. She was so excited for Baby Girl, and she was happy to be a part of her proud moment. Amiah helped her get in school and vowed to help her through every step. She truly believed in Baby Girl and wanted to help her any way she could.

"I'm more than ready. I'm ready to start my new life and start working toward my real career. I never thought I'd get this far, but I owe it all to you."

She smiled.

"You don't owe me a thing. If anything, you owe yourself. You deserve it."

The girls hugged and walked into the student center. As they waited, Amiah locked eyes with a familiar face. It was Braden. He was looking good, as always, but he wasn't dressed in his football uniform. He was wearing a pair of dark jeans, a button up plaid shirt that fit nicely on him, and a pair of Vans. He was dressed very casually and cleaned up in the face. Amiah smiled, and he walked over to her. Amiah stood up to meet him halfway.

"Hey, Braden. Long time, no see," Amiah said as they hugged.

"What's up, Miss Miah? I always see you, but you are always in a hurry, so I always say I'll catch you eventually."

They broke away from their hug.

"Yeah, school and my personal life keep me on the move. So, what's been up with you since school started?" Amiah asked.

"Nothing… just moved off campus and into my own apartment. I have few more weeks of school left, and then it's off to try and get drafted into the NFL!" Braden smiled widely.

"Oh my God, that's cool. Congrats. I still have two more years to go, but I've been doing this music thing to keep money in my pockets."

"Music? You must sing," he said with a smile.

"Yup, I sure do. My song is on the local radio station. It's called 'Loving a Hood Boy.'"

Braden stood back and looked at her with a look of shock.

"So, you are Ms. Bossy? My sister loves that song."

She smiled. Although she wanted nothing to do with Oxy, she

kept the name he had given her. She liked it, and the name was already established, so she saw no use in changing it.

"Yup, that's me."

"Well, I wasn't able to get your number at the party, so how about you give it to me now. Maybe we can go to dinner tonight if you are up for it."

Amiah thought about it for a second. It had been a couple weeks since her breakup, and she still thought about Oxy daily, but she wasn't going to call him or give any signs that she still cared about him. She knew, eventually, she would get over him. The night she went to the strip club with Bayley and Baby Girl, that made her realize she deserved to at least see what was out there. She knew there had to be somebody out there better than Oxy, so she decided to take Braden up on his offer with dinner just to feel him out.

"Sure… I'm free tonight, because the rest of my week is slammed."

Braden handed her his phone, and she put her number in it.

"Yeah, tonight is perfect. How's seven?"

She smiled.

"Seven is great."

The two hugged, and Braden walked off. Amiah walked back over to Baby Girl with a smile on her face.

"Girl, who was that?" Baby Girl said as she watched Braden walk off.

"A friend that's taking me to dinner tonight," she smirked.

"Okay, lovely. That's what's up. You deserve to find you some new peen."

The girls laughed. Baby Girl was right. She did deserve to find somebody else if she could. Then, she thought about how long she made Oxy wait. She made him wait all that time, and he still betrayed her. Therefore, she was going to try things different with Braden. She was going to take it slow, but not as slow as she did with Oxy.

***

Her date with Braden was everything. After she met him at his football practice and watched him play for a while, they went to dinner at a pizza parlor. They sat in there for three hours just talking, eating, and laughing. She got to know Braden very well. After she told him how she grew up, she found out how he grew up as well. She found out he was raised up north in Sacramento, and he was twenty-one. His major was philosophy, but he loved football. He didn't smoke, but occasionally drinks. Braden was the total opposite from Oxy. He dressed different, talked differently, and was taking a different path in life. She knew Oxy had changed his life, but she also knew he would always be a gangster and street nigga. Braden was not that. She was hoping Braden was something she could get used to, because she had gotten so used to Oxy and his ways.

"So, we've been talking about everything, but I never asked if you had a man."

Amiah smiled.

"Nope, I'm single."

"Well, I am too, so how about we change that."

Braden touched her hand and smiled. Amiah sipped her drink

and then smirked.

"We will see what happens as time goes by, but you can say I am yours."

Boldly, she reached over and kissed his soft lips. Amiah was going to do whatever she had to do to get over Oxy, even if it was just a kiss on the first date.

CHAPTER TWO

Life Changing

*M*eeze sat in his condo with a lot on his mind. Bayley was out shopping for Jamaica, so he decided to invite his boy over for a blunt and some conversation. Sitting in jail for a weekend really gave him time to sit down and think about what he wanted to do with his life. When he told Bayley he was opening a restaurant, he was serious. The way Oxy moved, it motivated him to want to do something other than robbing and slanging.

A lot of people didn't know it, but Meeze was a great cook and was always into culinary. He always said he would open a restaurant and be one of the cooks, but the street life made his dream become just that... a dream. Now that he finally had enough money saved up, he was ready to make that dream a reality. He had a child on the way and a child that he had never even seen before, so he wanted both his kids a part of his dream. He was going to find his baby and take him in. He knew Bayley would be pissed and probably try to leave him, but this was something he had to do. He was hoping once the situation was fully explained to Bayley, she would welcome his son into their lives, especially since Lucky would not be in the picture.

He was also excited about his upcoming trip to Jamaica. After he broke the news to Bayley and asked her if she wanted to go, she didn't have to think twice about saying yes. He was glad she agreed, because he had plans for them when they got there.

Meeze snapped out his thoughts when his phone started to ring. It was Oxy. He picked it up and answered.

"What's up, bro? I'm downstairs. Buzz me in," Oxy said through the phone. Meeze stood up and went to the intercom to buzz him in. A couple of minutes later, Oxy had walked in. The two of them slapped fives and flopped on the couch. Meeze had called Oxy over so that he could run down some things to him and get his opinion on it. He had so much in store, and he wanted to know if he was taking the right steps. He knew once he got his boy on board with his ideas, he would feel more confident about his business decisions and his decision about his kid.

"What's up, bro. I see you cut all that taco meat off ya face and head. Your ass was looking like that nappy headed nigga, Kevin Durant," Meeze joked as he pulled his tray of weed from under his coffee table. He never cared for another man's appearance, but his boy had been looking fucked up since his break up. He was glad to see him coming back together.

Oxy chuckled. He knew he had let himself go, but now that he was finally getting back organized, he was coming out of his misery. He still had Amiah on the brain, daily, but he knew he still had to take care of business so that he wouldn't go broke.

"Yeah, I just came from the barbershop just now. I got hella meetings this week. A nigga can't look like a bum forever."

Meeze nodded his head.

"So, I had you come through because I got a lot of shit going right now, bro. I'm ready to buy that restaurant I talked about as a kid, and I wanna get my son from that bitch, Lucky."

Oxy stroked his freshly shaved chin hair and nodded.

"What you need me to do?" he asked in a curious tone.

"I need you to help me get this info out the bitch so that I can get my kid. I was going to take him to my mama's house until I tell Bayley, but we gotta get rid of that bitch after we get him. Bay would never accept him if she knew Lucky was going to be in the picture with us."

Oxy nodded his head. He was down for whatever Meeze was talking about.

"I almost forgot about her. That bitch, Pricey, ain't called. I bet she is somewhere shook. We can go pay her a visit right now and see how much info we can get. If you want your lil' nigga, then we gon' get him, no questions asked. If that's your seed, then that means he's my nephew. I wanna be there for lil' man too. As far as your business, do that shit, bro. I can see you succeeding in that. You have always been a cooking ass nigga. I can hook you up with my lawyer. She does everything for me as far as business, so she can help you find the right spot and go over all the details on starting a business."

They both laughed a little, thinking back on all the times Meeze did his thing in the kitchen. When they were teenagers, Meeze would always cook for his family, and Oxy would be right over there with them, eating. He knew, eventually, his boy would finally break his street habits, and it was finally happening.

That was all the confirmation Meeze needed. With Oxy being on his side, he knew he could go forward with his plans. Oxy was a real business man. He knew he would help him with finding a spot and getting the paperwork done alongside his lawyer.

"Well, I ain't got shit to do 'til later. Bay said she won't be home until nine tonight. Let's ride over there and see what we can get," Meeze said as he lit up his blunt. The two of them smoked a blunt and then went off to the warehouse to see what they could get out of Lucky. If Meeze wanted her dead, that's what was going to happen.

***

They arrived at the warehouse thirty minutes later. When they walked in, it was dark, and the room reeked of urine. They both gagged when they walked in, and the smell hit their noses. The smell of piss only made them angry and ready to leave. Oxy walked over to the light panel and turned on all the lights. When they looked at Lucky, her eyes were closed. It had been a few weeks since they checked on her. She looked as if she had lost a lot of weight, and the clothes she had on had fallen off her from all the weight she lost. BR was supposed to send someone to feed her, but it looked like nobody had given her anything. There were a few bottles of empty waters on the floor, but they didn't know how long ago that was.

Meeze walked up to Lucky and stared at her. He reached over and checked her pulse. She was still alive. As he looked at her, he thought about the years they were together. They had been together on and off since high school. Since age fifteen, after he ran the streets at night,

Lucky was creeping across the street to his house through the back door. They had the same routine for years that they had gotten used to. Meeze knew he should have left her alone a long time ago, but her living right across the street from him just made her a convenience. He knew getting her pregnant was a mistake, and he knew he should have been careful, but he had gotten used to having unprotected sex with her as well. It was bound to happen, either way.

"Is she dead?" Oxy asked as he walked up to Meeze.

"Nah, she is still alive."

At that moment, Lucky opened her eyes. When she saw Oxy and Meeze, she woke all the way up. She frowned.

"Let me out of here, you bitch ass nigga," Lucky said, sounding weak. Her stomach was touching her back, and she was dehydrated. The whole time she was locked up, she had at least one bottle of water a day. They had some woman coming in that she had never seen before, giving her water like she was a dog. That's what she felt like... an abused and abandoned dog.

"So, are you ready to tell me where my son is and where that bitch, Pricey, is?" Meeze asked as he stood in front of her with his arms crossed. He couldn't believe that their relationship had to end like it was, but he didn't feel sorry for her. Lucky was a follower and always did what Pricey told her to do. Meeze always told her to stop hanging with Pricey, but since they were best friends, she thought everything Pricey did was right. Now, following under Pricey finally caught up to her.

"Fuck you, Meeze. If you want to know where that bitch, Pricey, is... I'll tell you, but you will not get my baby. You don't deserve him,"

Lucky cried out.

"What the fuck you mean? He's my kid, right? So, where is he, Lucky?" Meeze said in a gritty tone. Oxy charged up to Lucky and punched her in the mouth so hard that she was spitting blood and her bottom teeth.

"Bitch, your ass about to die, anyway. Tell my nigga where his kid is, or we will find your whole fucking family and murder them to get him. Do you want that to happen? Do you want your mama to die?" Oxy asked in almost a demonized tone. He wasn't there to play games with Lucky. He was ready to get his information and then off her ass.

"You think somebody is scared of you, Oxy? You ain't shit. You walk around here like you are some king, and you are not. Pricey may be scared of you, but I am not, so if you are going to kill me… do it, you woman beater!"

Oxy looked at her and frowned.

"Bitch, I am a king. That's why you bitches were on the run… because you were scared about what this king would do if I found you."

Oxy looked her deep into her eyes. Lucky was scared to death, but she continued to keep her guard up. Before Lucky knew it, Oxy was taking his fist to her face and punching her in the mouth over and over.

"Now, bitch, tell us where he is!"

"Okay!" she managed to say as she spat blood on herself.

"He's with my mother, and Pricey lives in Victorville now. 456 Jackson Street… apartment B. That's Pricey's address. My mother's new address is 2354 Normandie Ave… right across the way from her old house, Meeze. Now, please… don't hurt my son."

Oxy looked over at Meeze and smirked. Meeze smirked back. He put all the info into his notes on his phone and then walked behind Lucky. Meeze wrapped his arm around her neck and put her in a chokehold. Meeze squeezed tighter on her neck. He could feel himself taking all his pain and frustration out on the grip he had on her. Lucky gasped for air as Oxy watched Meeze choke her to death.

"Fuck this bitch," Meeze gripped harder on her neck and tilted it back. As Lucky stared at him, not being able to breathe, Meeze looked at Oxy, and he nodded his head in approval. Meeze turned her neck to the right as hard as he could, and snapped it. Once they heard the loud snapping sound, they knew she was dead. Meeze let her neck go, and her body went limp.

"This shit is finally almost over, bro," Oxy said as he walked toward the door.

"Yup… once we find that bitch, Pricey, this shit can be laid to rest. Now, I'm ready to go get my kid from her mom's crib."

The two of them walked out the warehouse, leaving Lucky's dead corpse behind.

"You gon' call somebody to clean that bitch up?" Meeze asked as they got in Oxy's truck.

"Yeah, I'mma let BR's crew take care of that, but I want to keep her body. I got something for that bitch, Pricey, when I catch that bitch. I want to bury those hoes together."

Meeze nodded his head. His mission was over as far as Lucky. When he found the right time to break the news to Bayley about his son, he could now throw in that Lucky was a non-factor, because she was dead. They left and headed straight to Lucky's mother's place.

***

Lucky's mother, Martha, had lived across the street from Meeze and his mother for thirty years, way before he was born. She knew his mother well and knew all about her daughter's dealing with Meeze. She repeatedly told her daughter not to get caught up in the streets, but she never listened. None of her kids listened, and it seemed almost impossible to get them out of her house. They disrespected her and her home so much. She had to move out and let them take over the home she lived in for so long. She moved not too far away, but it was far enough to get away from the bullshit her kids brought to her.

Martha ended up taking all six of her grandchildren in, including Lucky's new baby, N'mere, Jr. All she knew was that Lucky was in some kind of trouble, caught in drugs, and the baby also belonged to Meeze. That was all the information she was left with when Lucky brought the baby over to her with $1,000, a diaper bag, and some formula. After Lucky left, she knew she had no plans to come to get her baby.

Martha smiled at Meeze when she opened the door. Meeze smiled back, making sure he didn't come off as suspicious, just in case they found out about Lucky.

"How you doing, Miss Martha. Where is my son?" Meeze asked as he reached in for a hug.

"Oh, his little bad butt is in the living room in his playpen. I was wondering when you were going to stop by to see him," Martha said. She let him in and closed the door.

As Meeze and Martha walked toward the living room, Meeze started to feel a little nervous. This would be his first time seeing N'mere, Jr., and it kind of scared him. He had never feared anything, but all he could think about was what he was going to do with a child, especially a little boy. He had taken care of his sister's kids numerous times, but he knew having your own child was different. He wasn't even sure if he was ready to become a dad, but N'mere, Jr. was already born, and Bayley had a child on the way. He knew he had to man up and take care of his kids the right way.

When they walked into the living room, N'mere, Jr.'s eyes were glued to the TV as he clawed at the playpen, trying to lift up. He was too small to sit up by himself, but he tried. He was so active at four months.

"N'mere, stop clawing at that playpen, making all that noise. Look who's here to see you," Miss Martha said as if he could understand. She reached in to pick him up, and he started whining.

"Stop all that whining, with your spoiled butt. Your daddy is here to see you. This child looks so much like you. I remember when your mama first brought you home. You looked just like him."

Meeze smirked. Hearing Martha call the baby by his name made him think back on the baby pictures he had seen of himself. As soon as he had laid eyes on N'mere, Jr., there was no doubt that he was his. He had Lucky's light skin, but all his features and wavy hair had come from Meeze. He also knew that was his baby, because Lucky wasn't allowed to mess with any other dudes when she and Meeze were on good terms, and when she got pregnant, they were on good terms. That was the fuss of their whole relationship. Meeze had issues with double standards. He wanted to mess around with other girls, whether they were on good terms or not, but he wanted her to remain loyal.

"Don't be scared of him. Hold him."

Martha passed him over. Meeze took him into his arms and started rocking him gently.

"What's up, lil' man? I see you over here driving your grandma crazy."

Martha walked out of the room to give Meeze time with his son.

"I'm taking you with me. You are going to have a new family and a new life."

Meeze walked around the living room with his son and talked to him like a grown man. He wanted his son to know that he was safe with him and that he was his dad. Meeze knew he couldn't take him home yet, but he wanted him out of Martha's house, just in case she tried to give him up when she found out about Lucky. Until he got things situated, Meeze was taking him to his mother's. He knew she would be pissed, but he figured if he gave her some cash to take care of him, she would do it.

"Miss Martha, can you come here for a sec?" Meeze called out as he sat N'mere, Jr. in his playpen. Martha walked in with a smile.

"I want to take him with me for good."

Martha gave him a look of sadness. She walked over to the couch and sat down. She had become so attached to the baby that she didn't want him out of her sight.

"I don't know where his mother is. I keep having these dreams that she is dead. I pray for her every day, even though I know she is out doing dirt when she should be a mother to this baby. The last thing she told me was that you were the father. I've been trying to get in contact with you for the longest, but I don't know about you taking him."

"Don't trip. He is going to be fine. He's going to stay with my mom for a couple weeks, and then I'mma take him to my condo in the hills."

"Alright. I can't say no, because you are his father, but please don't keep him away from me."

"Don't trip, Miss Martha. I got you."

Meeze was never bringing his baby back to see Miss Martha. He wanted Bayley to be his mother and didn't want his son to know anything about Lucky. She didn't deserve to be a mother to him, especially since she chose the streets over her son. Therefore, he didn't even want his son to know her side of the family or know his mother in spirit.

Martha packed up his things and then sat him in his car seat. She helped him load up and helped him strap the baby in the backseat. She kissed his forehead and closed the door. Meeze got into the passenger seat, and Oxy drove off. As Oxy drove to Meeze's mother's house, he turned on the light and glanced at the baby in his rearview. He looked just like Meeze to him, but he still wasn't sure.

"He looks just like you, bro, but when you break the news to Bay, I think you gon' need more than looks to convince her."

"You think I should still do a DNA test?'

"Yup, to be on the safe side…"

Before they went to Meeze's mom's place, they pulled into Rite-Aid. Meeze rushed in for a DNA kit. When they got to his mother's, Meeze got the baby out the car. As he stood at the door with the car seat, he took a deep breath. He knew before his mom took the baby in, she was going to give him a hard time, but he was going to let her know that all of this was to better his life. He had so much in the works for his future and his family, and he wanted his mother to understand that. She had doubted him for a long time. Now, he was ready to prove her wrong. As soon as the door opened, she started going off on him.

"Oh, hell no, N'mere. You can't bring that baby here. Your sister already has me watching two of hers. Martha already called me and told me you took the baby. You might as well take him back to Martha's, because I ain't having it."

She puffed her cigarette and blew smoke into the air. Meeze smacked his lips.

"Mama, I just need your help for a little while. I am about to go to Jamaica, and when I come back, everything will be different. Can you at least just keep him until I come back and tell Bayley?"

Meeze was almost begging, and his mother could feel it. She looked at him with a side eye.

"Bring your ass in here, boy. I am so sick of you, your sister, and y'all kids."

She slammed the door. Meeze walked into the kitchen and sat the car seat on the table. His mom took the blanket from over the car seat and looked at the baby. She shook her head. The baby looked just like the N'mere she birthed. All her grandkids looked like her side of the family. They had strong genes, so she knew for a fact that was her grandson. She knew she couldn't tell her son no now that she had seen the baby. He had done so much for her, and she knew he was trying to change his life. Therefore, she was going to do it, but under her conditions.

"Dammit, N'mere. You got thirty days to get your shit together with Bayley, or I am taking him back to Martha's. You just told me she is pregnant. Now you have a baby by Lucky. I hope you have enough money for me to take care of him, N'mere, because I'm broke, taking care of Sharon's kids."

Thirty days was enough time for N'mere to go to Jamaica and break the news to Bayley. He had to come up with a way to break the news to her without upsetting her. He knew it was going to be hard, but he was taking his chances, because he really wanted a family with her.

"Alright, Mama… thirty days. I'm about to do a DNA test, just to be safe, and then I'm out."

"That's good, but the damn baby looks just like you. I'm not playing either, boy. If you don't come get him, he is back in Martha's care. He was doing just fine over there. If you weren't ready to have him, you should have kept him there."

"Alright, Mama. I hear you."

After he swabbed himself and the baby, he reached into his pocket and pulled out a wad of cash. He counted out five thousand and handed it to his mom. Elaine took the money and stuffed it into her bra. Meeze looked at his son one more time before he left.

***

After Oxy took Meeze back home to be with Bayley, he headed straight to Pricey's address. She lived two hours outside of LA, so he had a long drive ahead of him. Although he wasn't with Amiah, he still felt like he owed it to her to find Pricey and get revenge for what she did. He was still going to keep his promise, especially because Pricey deserved it anyway. Even before the incident with his son, Pricey was doing dirt. Money was coming up missing, and she was popping pills. She always claimed to be working late at the office, but she was really out being a whore. That's how he got so close to Baby Girl. She was the one he would confide in when he spent many nights in BR's strip club, selling pills, while Pricey did her thing as a whore. He was also with Baby Girl the night his son died, but he didn't tell her about it. He hadn't told too many people about the death of his son, because he didn't like women to feel sorry for him and see his weakness.

He knew he should have killed her a long time ago, but he knew he had his whole life to kill her, and now was the time. Oxy had a clear head that night. He had only smoked one blunt that day while he helped Meeze get his son. He also decided that he was going to cut down on drinking. He needed to get his head back in the game so he wouldn't get caught slipping by anybody or lose money. He loved Amiah and wanted to get her back, but he knew sitting around being depressed wasn't getting him anywhere. Therefore, it was back to business.

Two hours later, Oxy arrived at the address. It was a dark green apartment complex that almost looked like projects. He parked across the street from the building and got out. He walked across the street and zipped up his hoodie, putting his hood over his head. When he walked up to the gate, it didn't have a knob on it, giving him open access. As he walked through the dimly lit apartment building, he took his nine from his waist. After only walking a couple of feet, he spotted her apartment number.

When he walked up to the door, he could hear music playing. He looked over and saw the window was open next to the front door. He reached his hand through the blinds and opened it. When he walked in, he could smell incense mixed with the smell of cigarettes and crack smoke. He frowned up his face and walked down the hall with his pistol to his side. As he made his way down the hall, he could hear moaning. He knew for a fact that was her moaning. All Pricey knew was money and sex. Every time he thought about killing Pricey, his blood boiled. She was a whore, and she was grimy. To Oxy, those kinds of people didn't deserve life.

Oxy walked into the room and saw a man fucking the brains out of Pricey from the back. Oxy walked up to the bed and pistol whipped the dude in the back of the head so hard that he fell off the bed, sleep.

"Oh my God!" the woman turned around and said, trying to cover up her naked body. She was not Pricey, and Oxy didn't know who she was. Oxy walked up to the woman and grabbed her by the throat.

"Where the fuck is Pricey, bitch?" Oxy said in a gritty tone. He was angry the woman was not Pricey. He had a feeling she was on the run, again.

"Pricey? I don't know who that is. I just moved here a week ago," the woman said in a scared tone.

"Bitch, you better not be lying."

Oxy looked her deep in the eyes. He could tell the woman was scared to death.

"I swear, I don't," the woman began to cry. Oxy let her go and sprinted out of the house. He was angry Pricey wasn't there, but he should have known. Pricey was scary and didn't own up to anything she did. Oxy was so angry. He was ready to go after her family. He was sick of looking for her and sick of playing games, so he was putting it on his to-do list to murder her family.

As he rode back to the city, he decided he didn't even want to drive to the hills to his home. He was tired and overwhelmed. All he wanted to do was chill alone and get his mind right. Oxy drove to the nearest luxury hotel and pulled in to valet his car. Oxy had been spending a lot of money on hotels and rented luxury cars. He felt empty without Amiah, so making big purchases became his new love. When he walked into the hotel lobby, he laid eyes on Coby. He was hugged up with a woman in a red mini dress, waiting on the elevator.

"I'm finna murk this nigga," Oxy said as he pulled up the straps on his backup. When Coby laid eyes on Oxy, walking toward him with a mean mug on his face, he froze. After not being able to find him the night he went looking for him, he decided to just lay low on catching up with Oxy and be with his many women. He had turned into an alcoholic, a sex addict, and was A-wall from the military.

He wasn't even strapped, so he pushed the woman he was with and started running toward the emergency exit. Oxy chased right behind him with his hoodie over his head. He pulled his gun from his waist and started shooting at Coby as he ran as fast as he could. When Coby got to the second flight of stairs, he stumbled and fell down the flight of stairs. Oxy watched him roll down the metal steps, moaning and groaning from pain. When he got to the bottom of the stairs, Oxy ran down and stood over him. He bent down and turned Coby over.

"I thought you were going to kill me, you bitch ass nigga?" Oxy said, sounding out of breath, but he still had a devious smirk on his face. Coby was definitely at the wrong place at the wrong time. Oxy was already furious that he couldn't get Pricey, so he was definitely not sparing Coby his life. When Coby put that gun to his face and then actually tried to kill him, he wasn't giving any passes.

"Fuck you, you lil' mark. Shoot me, pussy. Amiah gon' leave your silly ass when she finds out… watch!" Coby shouted with blood coming out of his mouth.

"She already left me, bitch boy."

Oxy let off two shots to his head, killing him instantly. Oxy tucked his gun in his backpack. Thankfully, the stairway didn't have any cameras, but he quickly got his car from valet and found him another hotel to sleep in.

CHAPTER THREE

Jamaica

Oxy, BR and his girl, Leah, and Meeze and Bayley sat in a private airport, waiting for their private jet to be ready for them to board. After all the work Meeze, BR, and Oxy had put in over the last year, they were all more than happy to be getting away from California and spending four days in Jamaica. Each of them wanted to leave their lives behind and enjoy the tropical atmosphere. Meeze and Bayley decided on just relaxing and working on their relationship. Oxy decided to relax and get organized again. BR was just happy to be getting home to check on his business and his house in Jamaica.

Oxy sat in the lobby of the airport with his Bluetooth headset in his ears, listening to music. Bayley looked over at him as he bobbed his head to the music with his eyes closed. He was slightly slouched over with his head down. She could tell he was in deep thought, but she figured she could use this time to find out what was up with him and why he did what he did.

Every time she was with Amiah, they both talked about what happened, and Amiah never understood why he cheated. Bayley wanted to know if he was in a relationship with the girl he cheated with and what he was going to do to fix it. She liked Oxy for Amiah, and she also was a little more experienced in the bedroom as well. She knew if a nigga got his dick sucked for an hour and didn't fuck, he had no plans on fucking in the future. Amiah called herself dating, but Bayley knew she was only trying to heal her broken heart. Bayley felt there was room for them to maybe get back together, but only after she had a long talk with him.

While BR and Meeze walked over to get food, Bayley slid next to Oxy and pulled one of his earphones out of his ear, snapping him out of his thoughts. He looked over at Bayley and smiled.

"What's up, Bay? It's time to board?"

Bayley looked at him with her chin resting on her fist. She had a serious look on her face.

"No, we need to talk. I know you miss my best friend, and she misses you too, but she won't take you back, because you got your dick sucked. That really hurt her. Why did you even do it?"

Oxy took his headset off and sighed. He wasn't expecting to talk about Amiah to Bayley. Every time he thought about her, he felt so empty, so he tried his hardest to not think of her at all.

"Look, if you came to chew a nigga out for what he did, you might as well slide back over there. I know I fucked up. I live with that shit every day."

"I didn't come over here to chew you out. I just wanted you to know my best friend isn't built for those bullshit games you and Meeze try to play. Y'all wanted to have top notch bitches on y'all team but still want to mess with bottom feeder bitches, and that's wrong."

She shook her head.

"I love, Amiah, and I'll do anything to get her back. When I fucked around with my receptionist, I was in a fucked-up place with Miah. After her mom died, she shut me out. I tried to be there for her, but she told me she needed time to deal with it on her own. I would send her flowers, send her gifts, call her every day, but she told me she didn't have time for us and wanted to focus on school, work, and no sex. I filled up my schedule just like she did with hers, and when Erica came on to me, I cracked."

Bayley shook her head. She knew Oxy didn't mean any harm, and she also knew he was a man. Amiah was green when it came to pleasing her man, so she knew exactly what was going on. She felt bad for Oxy, and she was tired of both of them walking around like they didn't love each other. Therefore, she was putting her nose all in their relationship, whether they liked it or not.

"I want to help you get back with her, but it's not going to be easy. I'm not even going to let her know what is going on, but if y'all get back together and I have anything to do with it, you better not fuck up… even if ya dick is dry."

Oxy chuckled and nodded his head.

"You got it, Bayley. Can you at least just tell her that I am sorry, and I miss her? A nigga is sick not having her on this vacation with me."

Bayley nodded.

"Me too. I know she would have loved to come, but I'll see what I can do, Brandon… no promises… and you can't bug me, because you know Miah finds out everything."

"Alright, Bay. I said you got it," he chuckled. Bayley lightly punched his arm and slid back over to her seat. She was happy to know that Oxy was open with her. Now, all she had to do was relay the message. She didn't tell Oxy, but Amiah had been seeing Braden. Bayley was going to put an end to that, because she knew Amiah was going to get bored fast with that schoolboy shit that Braden had going on. Under all of Amiah's soft skin, there was a thug inside of her. She was always down to fight. She loved hood niggas, and she understood the streets. That's why she liked Oxy, and Bayley knew that all too well.

***

When they stepped off the plane, the sun was shining, and the air was crisp. Bayley stepped off first with Meeze, Oxy, BR, and his girlfriend following behind. The sky caps rushed over to the bullet proof Denali with their bags and tossed them in the back. When they all got into the truck, the driver got in route to BR's mansion, but BR wanted to ride through his neighborhood first. He had a huge party set up on the beach, and he wanted all of his family and friends to come out and show Meeze and Oxy some love. As they got closer to their first destination, they all looked out the window at the raunchy neighborhood they were driving through.

"Wow, this place is grimier than Watts," Bayley said as she looked out the window at the dirt road and run down homes. People were walking around barefoot while kids played in the dirt.

"We're in Kingston, Jamaica. This is my hood," BR said as he got out of the truck and walked over to a group of guys and women. BR insisted they all get out, including Bayley, to meet some of his friends. They all showed each other love, and then BR gave them flyers to his beach party. BR was well respected in Kingston, especially since his dad was one the largest kingpins still living in the slums.

After they left his neighborhood, they drove out toward the beach. Within an hour, they pulled up to a huge white house that almost looked like the White House in Washington, D.C., but modern. The grass was freshly cut, and there were huge thick palm trees out front. Jamaican women were walking around, tending to the garden while armed men walked around securing the place. BR was a big deal in Jamaica, and people couldn't wait for him to slip. That's why BR established a life in California when he turned eighteen and made Jamaica his vacation spot.

"Wow, this place is huge!" Bayley said with excitement as she stepped out of the truck. She was mesmerized and felt like she was in a tropical dream.

"Yeah… your shit nice, bro. Your shit killing my house," Oxy said as he looked at the huge mansion. Oxy's house was big, but BR's was extravagant. BR's butlers came out and unloaded the car for them while his maids came out with cold drinks for them.

"Welcome to my home, mon. Do whatever you like. There are eight bedrooms. Pick whatever one you want, except the master bedroom. Once you get comfortable, come out to the backyard and have some food and drinks that my mother prepared. Then, we can go over all the shit I got planned for the week."

Everyone agreed and headed off to find their way around the house. After everyone wandered the house and found their room, they headed out to the backyard. As soon as some of BR's female family members spotted Bayley and Leah, they took them off into the garden and started asking them questions about the states, Bayley's pregnancy, and what kind of stuff they would like to make their stay a lovely one.

"We know who Leah belongs to, but which one is your man?" BR's aunt asked Bayley. Bay smiled.

"The one in the white tank top… that's my man."

His aunt nodded her head.

"They all seem like good men, but I don't see a ring on your finger. Are you two talking about marriage?"

Bayley looked at BR's aunt. She really wasn't feeling all the relationship questions, seeing as she was only a guest, but she continued to answer her questions.

"We've been talking about it, but we have a lot going on in our lives."

"Well, you are a beautiful girl, and I know you understand love and life, because you are grown, but don't let that man knock you up again until he outs a ring on your finger. Like I told Leah, if a man loves you, his life will never be too busy to marry you. I wish both of you the best of luck, and I am praying for you and your baby."

Bayley nodded her head. Although she didn't know the woman, she was going to take her advice into consideration. She loved Meeze with everything she had, and she did want to get married to him, but she knew they weren't ready. Meeze wasn't even sure what he wanted to do with his life, and sometimes, she didn't even think they would last. She was just going to play her position as his woman and go from there.

"Thank you, miss. I will keep that in mind."

After the men finalized their meeting, everyone went into the house to feast on all of the food BR's mom had made for them.

***

The following night...

Meeze and Bayley were having the time of their lives, dancing to Jamaican music and feasting on Jamaican food. Curry goat, beef patties, rice, and other Jamaican dishes were on the menu, and they loved it.

"Are you and my lil' one enjoying yourselves?" Meeze asked as he stuffed rice into his mouth.

"Yup, I am. It feels really good to just get away from the city and be with my man," she smiled.

"Well, I'm glad you are relaxed and having a good time. I know I've been on some greedy shit, so I just wanted to make up for everything I've put you through…"

Bayley cut him off.

"Baby, I am over all of that. You have proven to me that you love me and care about me. You could have let me take the rap for that gun since I was the one driving, but you man'd up," she smiled again.

"Yeah, but your ass still went to jail. Luckily, the judge threw the case out, with your crazy ass."

They both laughed.

"Well, when I heard that cop say you were going to jail, I was devastated. I already lost my dad, so I didn't want to lose you. I don't know how I would live if you got years in jail."

She softened up her face, and Meeze could see it. He grabbed her hand and made her stand up from her chair. He looked her up and down. She was looking beautiful in her white one piece bathing suit. She had a pink sheer bathing suit wrap covering her back and arms with pink sandals. She also had a pink flower behind her ear that she picked from BR's huge backyard with her natural hair flowing. Meeze felt like Bayley was a blessing in his life. He was at a point in his life to where he would do anything to keep her. That's why he was ready to make his next move.

"Let's go walk the beach and watch the sunset."

Bayley agreed. They walked out of the tent and onto the beach. The two walked in silence, holding hands as the waves brushed the shore.

"It's so beautiful out here. I wish we could stay," Bayley said in a sweet tone as she looked out at the sunset.

"I wish we could stay too, but let me ask you something."

The two of them stopped walking.

"What is it, babe?"

"Do you want to be with me... forever?" Meeze asked with a serious look on his face as he studied Bayley. He wanted to see her body movements to know if she was telling the truth.

"Of course. I've been trying to let you know that since my father died, but the real question is, do you want to be with me... forever?"

He took her hands into his and gazed into her eyes. It was as though he could see their future in her eyes.

"Bay, I want to be with you forever, and some. When I first got the chance to talk to you, I didn't know what was going to come from it. All I knew was that you were wife material, and I wanted you. I didn't know how to love you at first, but although you might not think so, you taught me so much about love and having feelings. You are a thoroughbred that was made for me. Now, all I want to do is come home to your pregnant ass every night."

Bayley blushed.

"Aww, baby."

She was on the verge of tears, and she was speechless. Meeze was showing his softer side, and she loved it. Meeze reached into the pocket of his camo shorts and pulled out a ring box. He then got down on one knee.

"Babe, what are you doing?" Bayley asked with happy tears falling from her eyes. She knew what he was doing. She just couldn't believe they had made it to this point. They had been through so much. She thought she would never see him down on one knee.

"I'm proposing to you, lil' mama. Would you marry me?" he smiled and opened the box, exposing a beautiful diamond ring.

"Wow! I mean, yes. Yes, I'll marry you, N'mere!" she said with excitement. Meeze slid the ring on her finger. He stood up, and the two began to hug and kiss until the sun went down. Meeze was so happy that she accepted, and he was going to do everything to keep her and their baby happy. Now, he had to find a way to tell her about his other child. He really wanted his son to be a part of their family, and when the time was right, he was going to let her know.

The two of them walked back into the tent, and it was more live than it was before they left. BR was on the dance floor with Leah grinding on him, and Oxy was tipsy off the Jamaica rum he was drinking while talking to two fat booty Jamaican girls that BR had sent his way. When Oxy spotted Bayley and Meeze, he said a few words to the women and then walked over to them with a smile on his face.

"What's good, bro? Y'all having a good time?" Oxy asked with a huge smile on his face. He was feeling good, well rested, and stress free.

"Yup! I just proposed to Bay on the beach, and she said yes."

Bayley flashed her ring in front of Oxy's face. Meeze didn't tell anyone that he was going out to buy a ring to propose to Bayley. It was something he decided on his own, so this was going to be a surprise to everyone. Oxy's eyes grew widely.

"Congrats, bro! That's what's up!"

Oxy was genuinely happy for Meeze and Bayley. He knew they loved each other to death, so it was bound to happen. They slapped fives, and Oxy gave Bayley a hug.

"Well, fuck it. Let's celebrate with a drink and one of those fat ass Jamaican joints BR gave us. My nigga is about to be a married man. I can't believe it."

Meeze was with it. He was feeling good about taking things to the next level with Bayley, so a celebration was much needed. He hugged

Bayley and told her he would come back to her in a little bit. He and Oxy merged to the other side of the tent to have a smoke.

***

"What y'all just sitting there for? Start kissing or something," Oxy said as he blew smoke from his nose. BR had hooked him up with two sexy Jamaican females, and he insisted Oxy took them down at the same time. He had never had a threesome before, but BR kept pressuring him to have a good time before he went back to the states and to take the girls to his room in his mansion. Oxy gave in and took him up on his offer. He was single anyway, so he decided to enjoy it.

The girls looked at each other and smiled. They had never had sex with an American before, so it made them a little bashful. Before Oxy knew it, the girls had tied tongues with each other. Oxy sat at the edge of the huge king sized bed. The bed looked like a bed that needed to be in a king's palace with the gold trimming of it and huge gold headboard. The room was dimly lit with sex on the beach oil burning to kill the strong weed smell. As he watched them tie tongues and rub on each other's breasts while sitting next to each other in their G-strings, it made Oxy's nine inches get rock hard.

"Fi yuh, chocolate skin. Want to suck fi yutt dick," the woman said, speaking in Patois. The girls giggled.

"Yo, what your home girl just say?" Oxy asked in a dragging tone. He didn't understand anything she was saying.

"She said your chocolate skin is sexy like the men in our hometown, and… she wants to suck your dick," the woman that spoke English said to Oxy. Oxy chuckled and nodded his head. He reached over and sat his joint in the ashtray next to him and then put it on the floor. He stood up and walked over to the women. They wasted no time stripping Oxy down to his boxer briefs and tank top. The women pulled out his bulging penis through the peak of his boxers. Oxy had one catering to his stick and one catering to his nuts. He let out a sexy grunt as the women blew his mind. The women stood up and walked Oxy over to the bed. One woman laid on her back, and the other woman started going down on her friend. Oxy reached over to the nightstand and grabbed one of the magnum condoms. He opened it and slid it on his dick. He slid his stick slowly inside of her, making sure she could take all of him. She let out a sexy moan while she wiggled her ass, making sure all of Oxy's dick was inside of her.

The three of them were having a good time. The women were catering to all of Oxy's sexual needs, and he loved it, but he promised himself when he got back to the states that he was going cold turkey on pussy. He was going to continue to focus on his business and try and get right with Amiah. He knew she was angry and hurt. He also knew she was enjoying doing her, because he looked on her Instagram all the time. He wasn't going to let anything stop him from getting her back… not even another nigga.

***

Amiah and Bayley sat in the nail salon getting manicures and pedicures. Amiah was so excited to hear what happened on her trip to Jamaica. Bayley had told her something special happened, but she didn't want to tell her over the phone. Her engagement to Meeze was something that needed to be shared in person.

"Okay, bitch. You have been quiet the whole time we've been waiting here. What's the special thing that happened?" Amiah said with urgency. Bayley looked over at her and flashed her ring in her face.

"N'mere proposed."

Amiah smiled.

"Damn, bestie. Congrats. I see N'mere is stepping it up with y'all."

"Yup, he is. It was so beautiful. The sun was setting and all when he did it."

Amiah looked at her in awe.

"Damn, that's love. I am so happy for y'all. So, what else happened? What did y'all do?"

"We went swimming, sightseeing, and we did a little shopping. Oh, and guess who was there?" Bayley said, ready to spill it about Oxy.

"Who?"

"Your boo, Brandon. We had a long talk too. He said he loves you and misses you. I truly think he's sorry for what he did. Meeze told me he's been fucked up over you. He's been drinking… a lot."

Bayley was trying to get Amiah to feel sorry for Oxy, but it was not working, especially with the uninterested look on her face. She had been spending a lot of time with Braden, trying to not think about Oxy, and here Bayley was bringing him up. Hearing his name had messed up her perfect day. She looked at Bayley with much attitude. Amiah shook her head.

"Don't do that, best friend. I know what you are doing," Amiah said in a suspicious tone.

"What? Why don't you just talk to him and hear him out? I really think y'all should get back together."

"When or if I give Oxy another chance, it will be on my own terms, not yours or his. Your opinion on our relationship doesn't matter..."

Amiah put her attention to her phone. She didn't want to talk about Oxy to Bayley anymore. They were best friends, but she did not want Bayley thinking she was the one in control of her relationships. She was going to talk to Oxy when she felt like it, which was no time soon.

"Whatever, bitch. I was just trying to help."

Bayley rolled her eyes and stood to go get her color for her toes. She was mad that Amiah snapped at her when she felt like she was only trying to help. She knew Amiah was still mad at Oxy, but she wasn't giving up. She was still going to be in their business whether Amiah liked it or not.

CHAPTER FOUR

I don't belong to you

*E*rica was lying in her hospital bed, looking up at the TV. She was finally feeling a little better after being shot in the stomach and shoulder. She now had to use a colostomy bag, and all she could have was soup and puréed foods. The doctor said it would be another four months before she was able to use the restroom on her own, so it had her really down in the dumps. All she could remember was Oxy breaking things off with her and firing her. Then when they left, gunshots started ringing out. She hadn't even had time to heal her heart, because she was too busy trying to heal her body physically. She didn't even want to call Oxy, because she knew he didn't want anything to do with her. She figured that once she was healed, she would use one of her many degrees and put it to use to find a good paying office job.

As she was lying there in the dimly lit hospital room, she heard someone coming in her door. When she looked to see who it was, it was Emanuel and some woman. The two of them looked as though they were twins, so Erica assumed they were related.

"What's up, Erica? I heard what happened to you, so I thought I'd stop by," Emanuel said with a smile on his face.

"What the fuck do you want, Emanuel? I don't even feel like seeing you right now… or ever," Erica said with much attitude.

"Look, he just came to let you know that you need to stay the fuck away from that nigga, Oxy. He is crazy and trying to kill me, and if you are in the crossfire, you will be shot again," Pricey said, getting straight to the point. She didn't even feel comfortable being there to see Erica, because she didn't know if Oxy was going to show up, but her brother insisted she went everywhere with him for her safety.

"And? Who the fuck are you?" Erica said with an attitude.

"I'm Emanuel's sister, Pricey. That's who I am," Pricey shot at her.

"Are you are trying to say that you shot me, Emanuel? You came here to say you fucking shot me?" Erica shouted.

"I'm going to be on the outside of the room. I'm going to let y'all talk," Pricey said. She was not in the mood to hear them argue. She was ready to go. Every time she thought about Oxy being after her, her paranoia started kicking in.

"Look, Erica… it wasn't like that. You were just caught in the crossfire. If you want me to help you heal, here is my address. Call me when you get the word that you can leave. I'll protect you. If you come home with me, you won't have to worry about being in the crossfire again."

"Get the fuck out, Emanuel. Just go!" Erica shouted. Stupid Emanuel… he didn't know what he had gotten himself into. Once Emanuel left out of the door, she quickly reached for her phone and called Oxy's number. She knew he didn't want to talk to her, but she had to let him know what was going on. She couldn't believe Emanuel was trying to kill Brandon, and she wanted to warn him. She knew Emanuel would try his best to take Oxy down, especially since it had something to do with one of his siblings, but since he tried to kill her in the crossfire, she didn't care what happened to him. He didn't care about her enough to not shoot at Oxy while she was around.

Erica ended up calling him five times. Oxy finally answered his phone.

"Yo, who this?" Oxy said.

"This is Erica. I see you quickly deleted my number," Erica said in a weak sounding tone.

"It ain't even like that, Erica. What's good? You a'ight?"

"Actually, no… my ex came here with his sister, Pricey, saying they shot at us, and they want you dead."

"What?" Oxy shouted through the phone.

"Yup. That's what he came here and told me, and the stupid motherfucker left his address."

"Don't talk anymore. What hospital are you at?" Oxy asked.

"I'm at Kaiser Hospital on Sunset Boulevard."

"Alright, I'm on my way."

Oxy quickly hung up. Erica laid back in her bed and pulled the mirror from her hospital bag they had given her. She brushed up her hair and sprayed on some fragrance they had in the bag. She looked a mess, but brushing her hair back into a ponytail did a little justice. She knew Oxy hated an ugly appearance, so she wanted to at least look decent and smell good. She was hoping, just maybe if he saw her in a hospital bed, he would feel sorry for her and take her back. She was actually happy he was coming. She just wanted to see his face.

Thirty minutes later, Oxy was walking into Erica's room. When she saw his face, she wanted to cry. She missed him so much, but she knew that would only annoy him, so she tried to keep calm as much as she could.

Oxy walked in and stood over her bed. He was only there to get the address and go. He was done chasing Pricey around. He was ready to get her and whatever punk nigga that was saving her.

"So, where's the address?" Oxy asked with his arms folded, looking at Erica with a serious look.

"Hi, Brandon. I'm okay. What about you? Haven't seen you since all of this shit happened."

Erica knew she was pushing her limit, but she was a little angry that he just walked in asking for an address and not asking how she was doing.

"Look, Erica... this is some serious shit that has nothing to do with you. I didn't come here for the bullshit, so just give me the address so that I can go," Oxy said in an agitated tone. He wasn't trying to argue with Erica, because they had already settled that, it was over between them.

"All I ever was to you was a toy and a fucking slave. I did all your work and sucked your dick, and you treat me like this because you got caught? Fuck you, Brandon. Take the address and go. I don't want to ever see you again... ever!" she shouted, tossing the address to the foot of the bed. Oxy picked it up and stuffed it in his hoodie pocket.

"I can't fucking do this right now. I thought we agreed we were done. You knew what we had in the beginning. Remember… you are the one who came on to me and knew I had a girlfriend. I'm out."

He turned and walked away. Any other time, he would care that he had hurt her feelings, but it was over between them. He didn't have to take her feelings into consideration anymore. She was not his girl.

As Oxy was heading out the door, he bumped into a girl that looked just like Erica. He brushed it off and continued his route out of the door.

Erica's twin sister, Airys, had flown down from New York to finally see how she was doing. Airys had moved away from California when she started her life as a fashion designer. She always told her sister to come to New York and start over, but she never listened. Even though they were twins, they were total opposites. Airys was strong minded, and she was married while her sister continued to bust her ass in school and deal with no good men. Erica had enough degrees to live her life and find a decent man, but she'd rather settle for less and drown herself in school for no damn reason. She was always like that, and her sister hated it.

"Woah, sis. Who was that guy? He seemed mad," Airys said as she sat next to the bed.

"That was Brandon… the guy I was telling you about," Erica said as she wiped her tears away with a tissue.

"Oh my God, the guy that got you shot and was your boss? Well, what did he want? Did he apologize at least?" her sister asked with concern.

"No, he didn't apologize to me or even acknowledge that I am in pain. All he did was come get Emanuel's address that he left with me today."

Airys eyes opened widely.

"And, what is that creep coming up here for? You sure do mess with a lot of sickos, Erica. I don't even feel safe sitting here with you."

Airys stood up.

"Don't start judging, Airys. I am not in the position to be talked down on."

Airys shook her head.

"You always call it judging when I am trying to guide you. My flight leaves in one week, Erica. If you want to get away from the drama, call me before then so I can make arrangements for you to stay with me."

"I'm good, sis. I'll be just fine. Go on your little flight, and head back to your happy life."

Erica quickly brushed off her sister's presence and put her attention back on Oxy. She was truly disappointed in Oxy. She thought they were friends, and she thought he still cared about her, but clearly, his kind act was a fraud. Now, she wanted to find out what the beef was with Emanuel's sister and Brandon. Once she got a little piece of information, she was going to spread it around and make his life a living hell.

"You are the crazy twin, I swear. Well, since I am here, what did

Emanuel say when he was here?"

"Brandon is after Emanuel's sister for some reason, and I am going to find out why. Emanuel is the one that shot me, because he was shooting at Brandon. This shit is so crazy right now, but I'm madder at Brandon for not even considering my condition. I swear, when I get out of this place, I am going to make his life a living hell."

Airys shook her head.

"Sis, I've told you time and time again, if a man doesn't want you, leave him alone. Don't chase him. I really hate to say this, but if you don't get your life together, I am going to end up burying you, and I don't want to do that," Airys said in a sad tone.

"Nothing is going to happen to me. I am going to make Brandon pay... watch."

Airys shook her head.

"You are playing a dirty game with these men, and I don't want any parts of it. If you are going to stay here in California and mess up the rest of your life, don't bother calling me again, because clearly, you have your life all figured out."

Airys headed for the door.

"It's my life, and I do what I want. Now, you can leave."

Airys walked out the door. She was done listening to her sister talk crazy. She knew something bad was going to come out of Erica trying to get back at Brandon, and she wasn't going to stay around and watch it happen. She took a flight back home later that night, leaving her sister behind for good.

To Love & Die...

Oxy pulled up to the address he had gotten from Erica. He pulled in front of a huge house that was located in West LA. Oxy's blood was boiling as he exited his truck with the quickness and headed to the door. When he walked up, the curtains were open, and he could see Pricey sitting on the couch with a tray of cocaine in her lap. He shook his head. He then saw Emanuel walking into the living room with a beer in his hand. Nobody was even paying attention to Oxy in the window as he made himself visible. Oxy walked to the door and tapped on it with his gun.

"Who the fuck is it?" Emanuel said as he sat his beer on the table and walked to the door. When he opened it, he was presented with the barrel of Oxy's gun. His eyes lit up when he felt the cold barrel touch his temple. Before Emanuel could say anything else, Oxy let off his gun and blew his brains out. Pricey jumped up when she saw her brother hit the ground, but when she saw Oxy step in and close the door, she sat back down and started to cry.

"Oxy, please don't kill me. I am sorry. I am sorry for everything I put you through… even for what happened to our baby, but you have to understand that I loved you, and I was jealous once I heard you were dating Amiah. I felt like it just wasn't fair!" Pricey shouted.

"Bitch, shut the fuck up with all that fake ass pleading you like to do. Pick up that tray of dust. I want you to snort all of it," Oxy said in a gritty tone as he had his gun pointed at her. Pricey looked down at the tray of coke and shook her head. There was no way she could snort every line on there. The dope she had was to last her a couple of days. She knew if she snorted it all, she would be dead, and she knew that's what Oxy wanted.

"I can't snort all of this," Pricey said in a childlike tone with tears streaming down her face, but Oxy didn't feel anything for her. He tucked his gun and stormed over to her. He slapped her in the face so hard that she started seeing stars.

"Bitch, I said snort all of that shit, now!" Oxy demanded. He grabbed her by her weave and forced her to her knees.

"Start fucking snorting, bitch," he said in a gritty tone. Pricey plunged up her nose and snorted the first four lines. Pricey was still an amateur when it came to snorting coke, so those lines had her in a daze. Oxy looked on and smirked as Pricey tried her best to keep her eyes open. Her nose was dripping blood and snot.

"Oxy, please… I can't snort anymore. I feel like I am going to pass out," she cried out as she crawled onto the couch.

"Bitch, don't pass out yet. Let's go."

Oxy walked her out to the car and tossed her in the trunk. He got in route to the warehouse. As he drove there, he called his big home girl, Nikay. Nikay was like a big sister to him and would do anything for some cash. Nikay was six feet tall, 250 pounds, and she was a fighter. Oxy had an easy job for her, and he only had to give her a thousand dollars. He called her up.

"What's good, Ni? You gon' do that favor for me tonight?" Oxy asked.

"Yup, you know I got you, boo… long as you got that money."

"You know I got that money. I'm about to be on my way. I'm only fifteen minutes away."

The two dismissed their call. When Oxy pulled up in front of Nikay's house, she was already waiting outside. When she got in, Oxy drove off and headed to the warehouse. Nikay was dressed in a black sweat suit with her hair tied up. She was ready to beat the brakes off Pricey, and Pricey didn't even know it.

"Alright, Ni… I got a dead body laid out there, but it's embalmed, so it don't stink," Oxy warned Nikay about Lucky's dead body before she got there and got nervous. Nikay laughed.

"Boy, what? You crazy. A'ight… since a bitch gotta be heartless tonight, the shit is going to cost you more, nigga."

Oxy nodded his head.

"Money is no issue, and you know that, Ni."

When they pulled up and parked, Oxy opened his trunk and grabbed Pricey out by her messy hair. She was high and in a daze. But when she laid eyes on Oxy, she started crying again…but this time screaming. She didn't want to die. She felt like she didn't deserve it.

Oxy opened the door and pushed Pricey in. She fell to the floor, still screaming and crying. Oxy walked over to her and kicked her.

"Bitch, shut the fuck up. Don't nobody feel sorry for you. Stand the fuck up!" Oxy demanded.

"Nikay, lock the door, and get ready to square up with this punk bitch."

Oxy walked over to the body bag that was on the floor and unzipped it, revealing Lucky's corpse. Pricey saw her face and began to vomit on the floor.

"Oh my God! What did you do to her?" Pricey asked as she continued to gag.

"Yeeaahh, bitch. You thought this shit was a game. You like to fight? Well, fight her," Oxy said with a smirk on his face. As soon as Pricey turned around to face Nikay, Nikay punched her in the face, sending her stumbling. Pricey didn't want to fight. She was too high and too weak.

"Come on, bitch. Fight back!" Nikay shouted. Oxy stood back with his arms folded, getting a kick out of Nikay beating the hell out of Pricey. Pricey tried to swing as much as she could, but Nikay was dodging all of her hits. Nikay punched her everywhere until she fell to the floor. Nikay got on top of Pricey and started pounding her face with her fist and banging Pricey's head onto the ground. Nikay was bloody and trying to beat her to death which was her and Oxy's agreement. Nikay had done this plenty of times, so she didn't feel anything as she murdered Pricey. Nikay banged Pricey's head to the cement ground one more time, shattering Pricey's skull and killing her.

Nikay stood up. She was out of breath, and her sweatsuit was ruined. Oxy started clapping at the good ass whooping she had given Pricey. He felt like he was watching a women's UFC fight.

"Nice job, Ni. You definitely earned this three Gs," Oxy said as he passed her the money that was wrapping with a rubberband. She stuffed it in her bra and smiled.

"The way you told me that bitch treated you and your girl, I knew what kind of ass whooping I was going to give her, and she killed your baby. I wasn't feeling that. I've been knowing you since you were little, and you have always been a solid nigga, but that bitch is gone now. You don't have to worry about this bitch anymore."

Nikay kicked Pricey's bleeding corps. After Nikay helped Oxy stuff Pricey's body into the same body bag as Lucky, he laid plastic in his trunk and tossed the bodies in there. He then drove down to the Los Angeles River and dragged the bodies out into the woods area, near the water. After tossing them, Nikay and Oxy quickly headed back to his truck so that he could take Nikay home. He was finally feeling relieved now that he had demolished all of his enemies. He could move on with his life and only hope to not make any new enemies. He was also done with the murder game. He was done laying out bodies and wanted to retire his ways. That's why he didn't want to make any more enemies. He was now all about his money and his love life, because he was still confident that Amiah would eventually come back around.

CHAPTER FIVE

*A*miah and Braden held hands as he walked Amiah to her morning chemistry class. The two had been dating and studying together for the past month, and Amiah was feeling it a little. Braden was so sweet but a little overbearing. He was keeping her company. He wanted to walk her to class, meet her to study, and then do dinner every night. The two hadn't had sex, but a lot of fooling around and kissing was involved. Amiah liked that he didn't pressure her into sex. She didn't know how he was pleasing himself, and she never asked. Sometimes, she thought maybe no one was pleasing him, because he was always with her.

"So, where do you want to eat tonight?" Braden asked when they stopped in front of her class.

"I was thinking some Thai food. Yeah… let's get some Thai."

Braden turned up his nose.

"Nah, let's do Italian."

Amiah laughed and shook her head.

"You always do that. Why ask me where we are eating if you are not going to agree with what I want to eat?" Amiah said with a slight attitude, because Braden had been doing that a lot, and it kind of annoyed her.

"I was just looking for suggestions… not actually wanting you to choose. You always want to eat nasty healthy stuff," he laughed.

"Whatever, Braden… Italian is fine."

At that moment, Amiah's phone began to ring. When she looked at her phone, it was her family lawyer. She had been waiting for the money her mother left her to clear with the insurance company. She was hoping to get some good news, because she was ready to trade in the car Oxy gave her and move into her own apartment near the school. She was tired of her small space, and she was tired of riding around in a car that Oxy had gotten for her. The car was still in good shape, but she wanted something with her own money.

Amiah put her finger up to Braden so that he wouldn't talk when she answered.

"Hey, Michelle. Please tell me you have some good news for me," Amiah said with a smile.

"Hey, Amiah. I have good news and bad news. I am going to start with the bad news. Your brother is dead. Have you watched the news? He was found at the bottom of the stairs in the Beverly Hills Hotel's emergency stairway. He was shot to death a week ago."

Amiah shook her head. She knew eventually her brother was going to end up dead with his fucked-up ways. Her next thought was, *did Oxy do it? Did my brother push him to the limit enough to kill him?* She pushed her thoughts to the back and focused back on her lawyer on the phone.

"Oh, wow… I guess I have another funeral to plan. Well, what's the good news?"

Amiah started walking down the hall so that Braden wouldn't be in her business. There was a lot about her personal life he didn't know, and she wanted to keep it that way.

"Well, the good news is that you have enough money to do so and some. After I took my cut from the top like you asked, you ended up with one million. The insurance policy your mother had on your brother was in your name and hers as well. They both had a balance of 100,000 dollars."

Amiah's eyes lit up.

"Damn, where did my mommy get all this money from?" Amiah laughed. Her mother always lived like she didn't have any money, all the while she was sitting on some serious cash.

"She took out the best insurance policies for you three as soon as you guys were born. That's how. Your mother was a smart woman for doing this. Now, you can go on and live life the way you want. She also left you a letter in her safe deposit box that you need to read."

Amiah nodded her head.

"This is so crazy. I'll be down there so we can go over everything," Amiah said and quickly hung up the phone, walking back over by Braden.

"What's going on, pretty lady? Who has you smiling?" Braden asked.

"My lawyer... my brother just died, so I have to go handle that," she started walking off fast.

"Your brother died, and you are smiling? Well, do you want me to come with you?" he asked in a confused tone. He had never seen anyone as happy as Amiah when their brother died.

"This is personal, Braden. I'll meet you for dinner later."

Amiah rushed off and headed to her car. She got to her mother's lawyer's office in record time. She parked in front of the building and walked up to the receptionist desk. Michelle was already sitting at the front desk with the receptionist.

"Hey, Ms. Miah. I was just up here waiting for you. Let's head to my office."

Michelle stood up. She and Miah walked into her city view office. Michelle Davis, had been Linda's lawyer since her divorce with Amiah's father. She helped her get everything she felt she deserved from her ex-husband, and she also helped her manage her fat insurance policy she got for her and her kids. Once she found out she had cancer, would be battling it for a long time, and could possibly die, she wanted to secure her kids' futures, especially Amiah's. She got an even bigger insurance policy for them. She knew her daughter had goals. She wanted her to accomplish them and not let money be an issue. She wanted the same for Coby, but she knew he would die before Amiah, so she added Amiah as a beneficiary on his policy.

"So, basically... this is how it goes. I have a check for one million dollars for you. You need to go to Bank of America and deposit it. It will take a couple of weeks to clear, and if you owe anybody, they are going to take their cut, but here you go. I wish you the best."

Michelle slid her two envelopes. Amiah opened the envelope that had just her name on it. When she opened it, it was her mother's letter. She smiled when she saw her mother's handwriting. She had missed her so much, so getting a letter from her while she's gone truly made her feel good…

Sweet Amiah,

If you are reading this letter, I am long gone, but I want you to know you don't have to be sad about it. From the moment I birthed you, I knew you would be a smart girl. You were always ahead of your milestones and always did good in school. You had been singing since you were a baby, and I knew you would always be good at anything you did. That's why I left you so much money. I know you are responsible enough to do what's right with such a large amount of money. Start your cosmetic line, pursue your music career, have my grandkids, (laughing), and explore the world. Don't be like your brother. Get out that hood mentality, and make something of yourself.

I love you, baby girl.

Love, Mom.

Tears flooded Amiah's face after she read her mother's letter. She really missed her mother, and it tore her up every time she thought about her. She was so thankful that her mother had left her all that money, and she was going to do everything her mother told her to do.

Michelle passed Amiah a Kleenex box. She and Michelle said a few more words, and then Amiah headed straight to the bank with her mother on her heart and brain.

***

Two weeks later...

Amiah drove up to the Jaguar dealership with her own music bumping and wearing a pair of Dolce shades. She was in good spirits and ready to make some changes. She had been ripping and running all day and still had things to do. She had just come from dropping off her deposit on her brand-new condo in West LA. Now, she was at the dealership, trading her Benz in for a new 2015 Jaguar. Then, after she got her car, she was headed to her brother's memorial at the church. She decided to just cremate him and keep all the extra money. Her mother didn't even have a spot for him in the cemetery, and Amiah wasn't getting one for him. She felt like he didn't deserve an expensive funeral. Her greatest revenge on him was watching his body be turned into ashes.

Amiah pulled up and walked into the dealership. When she walked in, a cute black girl greeted her. She was wearing a red skirt that stopped at her knees and a black top. Her hair was curled, and she had on red lipstick, holding a clipboard.

"Welcome to Jaguar Los Angeles. My name is Elecia. Did you see something out there that you like already?" Elecia smiled.

"Yes, I sure did. I am feeling that new Jag out there in blue, and I'd like to pay for it in full," Amiah said with confidence. The car wasn't even half of how much money she had, not even her condo. She decided to continue to keep her life simple and comfortable as it was, and invest the rest of the money into her cosmetic line she was working on and her music career.

"That's what's up... so are you looking to trade in that pretty Benz you got out there, or are you keeping it?" Elecia asked. That was her usual question to every customer.

"Yup, I sure am. It just gives me too many memories of my ex, so it's time to upgrade already."

"I definitely understand that. Well, let's run your credit and get the paperwork going. Then, we can check the car out, and you can test drive it. I hope you have a couple of hours," Elecia said as she walked Amiah to her cubicle. Amiah looked at her gold watch and saw that it was already 2:30. Her brother's memorial started at 4:30. Amiah wasn't even worried about it. She continued with Elecia and sat down at her desk.

Amiah slid all the paperwork for the Benz and her driver's license to Elecia, and she immediately started giving Amiah papers to sign. Elecia looked over the paperwork and saw that the car was registered in Brandon's name.

Brandon Merrier, she thought to herself when she saw his name and Calabasas address. She wasn't all the way sure if it was Oxy, so she continued to type information into her computer. Then, she looked at Amiah and remembered seeing her face on Oxy's Instagram. He didn't have a lot of pictures of Amiah but enough for her to remember her face. Elecia thought back on the night he left her hanging and shook her head.

"What? Is something wrong with my credit?" Amiah asked in a worried tone when she noticed Elecia shaking her head.

"No, your credit is fine, but the car is registered in someone else's name, so we can't take it. Once you get the car in your name, we can take it... but let me ask you something. Are you Oxy's girlfriend?" Elecia asked, boldly.

"We're not together anymore. How did you know I was with him?" Amiah asked in a curious tone. She really didn't like how Elecia was asking her questions about Oxy. Elecia didn't want any problems with Amiah, because with her buying the car at full price, she was going to get a fat commission check, but she couldn't help but want to know her status with him.

"I never messed around with him or anything. I just saw your picture on his page. That's the only reason I asked. Y'all are cute together."

For some reason, Amiah smiled at her compliment.

"Thank you, but he is a thing of the past."

Elecia made it a mental note that he was single. She decided she would give him a call to see if he would like to make up for the night he had fallen asleep on her.

"Well, let's get back to this car," Elecia said, changing the subject back to business. Other than the bullshit Elecia was talking about with Oxy, Amiah was disappointed about not being able to do a trade in, but she still wanted her new car.

"Okay... that's fine about me not being able to trade in, but I still want to drive my Jag today. I can have my best friend pick up my car."

"That's cool," Elecia said, handing Amiah more paperwork. As soon as all the paperwork was done, Amiah test drove her new car and paid for it. Since she paid full price for it, they included a Jaguar car seat and some other nick-nacks for the car. Amiah decided to give Bayley the car seat. She then called Baby Girl and asked her to come get her car, and she agreed.

***

Amiah pulled into the church for her brother's memorial, and parked. There were cars parked everywhere with people walking up to the church to get inside. Amiah was thirty-minutes late and could care less. She was ready for the day to be over so that she could drive around in her new car with Baby Girl and Bayley. She needed to do some shopping for her new condo, and she wanted her best friends to help her pick out décor. Amiah got out her car and walked up to the church.

When she got to the front, her cousin, Stacy, was standing outside smoking a cigarette. Amiah truly didn't care too much for her cousin. She did help Amiah with her mother when she wasn't available and when she was in the hospital after Pricey jumped her, but she was getting paid. Every time she took care of Miss Linda, she got $300. Amiah knew if she wasn't getting paid, she wouldn't have been around. Amiah remembered the day her aunt Becca begged Stacy to come down and help Amiah and her mother. The only way her mother got her to say yes was when she brought up the pay. Amiah didn't know her cousin that well. All she knew was that she was her mother's niece that lived up north.

"You just ain't got no kind of respect. You show up thirty minutes late to your brother's funeral. You need to be ashamed," Stacy said and flicked ashes near Amiah's colorful Louboutin stilettos.

"Talk about respect from a bitch that's smoking a cancer stick in front of the church."

"Don't get cute, Miah. I know your mama left you all that money, and you didn't even bother to give me anything when I helped y'all… and I know your punk ass boyfriend killed my cousin. I am going to find out, and his ass is going to jail," Stacy said with confidence.

"The money my mother left me has nothing to do with you, and Brandon didn't have anything to do with this, Stacy. Coby had a lot of people that didn't like him. It could have been anyone. Now… you need to back up with that cigarette before we have a problem," Amiah said, giving Stacy a warning. Stacy was moving in close to her, and Amiah didn't like Stacy in her space.

"What is your stuck-up ass gon' do? You got some nerves being mad at me. I was the one taking care of your mother while you were laid up in a hotel, sucking some hood nigga's dick. You are just like the rest of the bitches in the hood. You ain't no saint, Miah—"

Before Stacy could say another word, Amiah punched her in the mouth. She came out of her heels and started pounding her fist into Stacy.

"Bitch, don't you ever mention my mother's name again. You didn't take care of shit! I did! You got paid, hoe!"

Amiah continued to beat on her until one of her uncles came to break it up.

"Y'all stop fighting. Stop fighting. Y'all are at Coby's memorial."

One of their uncles finally got them pulled apart.

"Fuck you, Miah. I don't want to ever see you again, bitch. You ain't my fucking family!" Stacy shouted as her uncle dragged her into the church.

"Bitch, that's an easy call… with your hood rat ass!"

Amiah picked up her heels and put them back on. She then walked off to her car and got in to finish off her day. She was not interested in being around her fake ass family for a man that she cared nothing about. She headed out of the parking lot and headed to meet up with Baby Girl and Bayley for a night of shopping. She didn't need her family. She had her girls. That was her only family.

CHAPTER SIX

$\mathcal{S}$tand the $\mathcal{R}$ain...

$\mathcal{A}$miah rushed around the backyard of the mansion she had rented out for Bayley's baby shower. Bayley was now seven months pregnant and finally revealed that she was having a girl two weeks prior. Amiah was so ecstatic when she heard the news, so she immediately put together a nice baby shower for her god baby. Bayley invited her close family, and Meeze did the same, leaving Amiah to entertain at least eighty people. Everyone was advised to wear all white with a little bit of hot pink, and everyone followed the dress code, even the men.

Bayley, Amiah, and Baby Girl wore white sundresses with matching hot pink accessories. Bayley was so excited and so was Meeze as they greeted all their family members that walked through the side gate that led to the back yard.

"Best friend, everything turned out so nice. I love the decorations," Bayley walked over and said.

"I knew you would love it. I even got the diaper cake just like you asked," Amiah smiled. The girls hugged.

"Thank you so much for everything. This wouldn't have been a success without you. Now, you can do that for your god baby's first birthday too... and my wedding," Bayley laughed.

"Nah, I'll leave that one up to you and N'mere."

As the girls chatted for a while, Amiah immediately became distracted when she saw Oxy walk through the side entrance with a hand full of silver and pink gift bags. He was wearing some white Levi's, a white button up shirt, a pair of Nike Air Max's with a hot pink Nike sign, and a rose gold rope chain, following the dress code. He wasn't wearing a hat, so he was showing off his fresh cut and shaved beard he had grown. Amiah couldn't lie. He was looking good, but she wasn't going to show any interest in him.

"What is he doing here?" Amiah said through clenched teeth as she watched him walk over to the gift table and sit his gifts down. Bayley looked at Amiah with a cheesy smile. She knew Oxy was coming, but she wasn't going to dare tell Amiah. She would have flipped out and probably canceled the baby shower, and Bayley didn't want that to happen.

"Becaauussee, he's N'mere's best friend... remember? How can we not invite him? Plus, I just found out today he was coming," she laughed, but Amiah didn't find anything funny.

"I'm going inside to open a bottle of wine. You knew he was coming. I know you knew well before today that this fool was coming."

Amiah rushed off into the house. Seeing Oxy only brought back memories of them together and memories of him cheating on her with Erica. She didn't want her thoughts and emotions to ruin her day, so a glass of wine was much needed. She walked into the kitchen and grabbed one of the bottles of Stella Rosa from the counter. She used the corkscrew on the counter to open it. She then filled her wine glass to the top. She walked over to the sink and gazed out the kitchen window, looking at all the guest walk through the back. As she sipped her wine, she felt a pair of hands on her waist.

"How you been, Miah?" Oxy said in a low tone near her ear. It had been a long time since she felt his touch and heard his voice, so he startled her a little. She sat her glass down on the window seal.

"What do you want, Oxy?"

"I want you to talk to me, babe. Can we talk?"

Amiah turned around to look him in the face. He was so close to her, she could smell his icebreaker mints sitting on his tongue.

"You need to back up, and I am not your babe," Miah said in an uninterested tone, putting her hand in his face. He was just too close. She tried to escape from him, but he had both hands on the sink, trapping her in.

"Have you been getting the flowers I've been sending to your dorm?" Oxy asked. He could care less about being in her space. He needed her back, and he wasn't backing down just yet.

"No, I moved out my dorm, so you have been sending them to my old roommate. Now, move."

"Look, Miah. I'm sorry, and I love you. I think about you every day, and I regret the shit I did to you. Can you forgive me?"

Amiah looked off in space so that she wouldn't have to look at him anymore. She crossed her arms, trying to be strong. Having him in her space made her want him, but she was not ready to give in. Oxy was dead wrong for what he did, so to her, he deserved to be dissed.

"You weren't thinking about me when you were getting your dick sucked, so don't think about me now, or ever."

He frowned.

"Dammit, Miah. What do I have to do to prove to you that I am sorry?" he asked in an aggravated tone.

"Take back what you did… oh wait… you can't. That's something that can't be undone, *Oxy*. Now, I'm going to need you to leave. I have guests to attend to," she shot at him. She was so mad that she could feel her blood boiling. Oxy stepped back and looked at her. He was so mad at the way she was treating him that he just wanted to grab her and shake her, but he decided to leave it alone.

"You want me to leave, huh. Okay, I'm leaving… since you don't want a nigga here."

"My nigga, Oxy… what's the deal, bro? I have been looking all over this bitch for you," Meeze said in a loud tone, throwing them out their staredown. Oxy turned around, and Amiah turned around to finish her wine and get her mind back on the baby shower as if he was never there. Oxy walked over to Meeze, and they walked into the living room. The two gave each other pounds.

"What's good, bro? I'm about to bounce. I left my gifts on the table. I'll get up with you later," Oxy said as he headed toward the front door.

"Leavin'? You just got here, my nigga. I thought we were gon' smoke this blunt and drink this Henny," Meeze said in a confused tone. He had been waiting three hours for Oxy so that they could turn up while the women did their baby shower thing, but Oxy was bailing out on him.

"Ya stuck up host over there doesn't want me here, so we can meet up later at the crib. Text me, bro."

Oxy walked off. Meeze shook his head.

"Damn… fa sho', bro. I'mma hit you."

Meeze walked off with his blunt and his bottle of Hennessy and wandered around the house until he found one of the bedrooms. The room was empty, so he opened the blinds and sat on the carpet near the window. He was over Amiah and Oxy's broken relationship. He couldn't wait until his boy got back with her or found another woman, because he was tired of them going back and forth and getting nowhere.

***

Bayley sat at one of the tables with her feet propped up on a chair. That was the one thing she hated about her pregnancy was that she had swollen feet if she stood too long. She couldn't wait for her last few weeks to be up, because she was ready to have her baby and get her body back, even though she decided to breastfeed. She had played all the games, ate as much as she could, and opened all her gifts with Meeze. Now, all she wanted to do was pack up and go get in her bed.

"Here, girl. I know you're ready to drop my grand baby, because you look worn out!" Meeze's mother, Elaine, said as she handed Bayley some ice-cold water.

As of late, Elaine and Bayley had become close and began a

mother-daughter relationship. Elaine knew Bayley didn't have a mother or father, so she didn't mind taking her in as one of her kids. She had a funny feeling about Bayley in the beginning because she was so young, but she had a change of heart once she found out about Bayley being pregnant and holding her son down to the fullest. She knew Bayley was the reason for his life changes, and she respected and loved it.

"Thank you, Mama. Yes, I am more than ready."

Elaine sat in the chair next to Bayley. She was holding one of her grandkids all day. Bayley couldn't keep her eyes off the baby boy she had glued to her hip. His eyes were so familiar, but she couldn't put a finger on it. Bayley reached over and shook his little hand.

"Mama, I been meaning to ask you all day… whose baby is this? He is too cute," Bayley said with a smile. She then started talking in baby talk to the baby boy, and he started smiling.

"Girl, this is N'mere's damn baby. He ain't told you yet? That nigga had thirty days to tell you, and his time is up!" Elaine said. She had been drinking, so her mouth was running like water. Bayley looked at the baby and then looked at Elaine. She felt like her heart had stopped, especially since the baby looked just like Meeze's baby pictures but had lighter skin.

"Are you serious right now, Mama?" Bayley asked in a confused tone. She could feel her blood boiling, but she kept her cool. At that moment, Meeze walked up and stood next to his mama.

"What's up, Mama. You ready to go?" Meeze asked.

"So… this yo' baby, N'mere… for real? You got a secret baby?"

Bayley looked at him with eyes of death. She wanted to fight him at that point, but she continued to keep her cool. Meeze looked at his mama and frowned.

"Damn, Mama. Why you say something? I told you that I was going to tell her."

"Nigga, I had this baby for almost two months, and that money is gone. I told you, I'm not running a foster home. You need to get your baby tonight and go be a family with Bayley... or drop him off at Martha's," she expressed with much attitude. Elaine was truly tired of taking care of kids. She had already raised her own. Now, it was time for her kids to do the same. Bayley stood up on her swollen feet and slid her flip flops on.

"Oh, hell no! This nigga going to send me into early labor. Are you fucking serious right now?!" Bayley shouted. Amiah was standing off, talking to Baby Girl, and heard Bayley yelling. She told Baby Girl to stay to the side, and Amiah walked over to Bayley and Meeze.

"Is everything okay, best friend?" Amiah asked with a concerned look.

"Yeah, I'm good. I'll let you know later what the fuck is going on with this fuck nigga right here," Bayley said in disgust. She could hardly look at him.

"Yeah, she's good, Amiah. This ain't yo' issue, my nigga, so go back to what you were doing," Meeze said in a slightly irritated tone. He knew shit was about to hit the fan, so he was mad at everybody, especially his mother. She was the one that started it all up.

"This has all of everything to do with, Amiah, because she is my best friend. If she wants to know what's up, I'm going to tell her."

Bayley was ready to cause a scene, but Amiah was so confused. She couldn't have her back if she didn't know what was going on.

"Hold up. This shit ain't got nothing to do with her. All she needs to worry about is how she gon' get right with that nigga, Oxy. That's the only business she got."

Amiah frowned up her face and shook her head.

"Hold up, N'mere. Don't snap at me, because I don't know what is going on. Oxy and I have nothing to do with this. Handle your nigga, Bay!"

"Y'all need to go somewhere and talk. Y'all making this baby upset," Elaine said as she watched N'mere, Jr. start up his usual crying. Meeze grabbed Bayley by the arm and stormed into the house with her. He walked her up the stairs as she cursed and yelled at him. Meeze opened the room door he was in earlier and closed it.

"Let me the fuck out of here. How could you do this to me? A baby? Really, N'mere! By who? By fucking you? We're supposed to get married, and you got a bitch pregnant?" she shouted with tears streaming from her eyes. She was so hurt. She thought their daughter was his first child, and clearly, it wasn't.

Meeze stood in front of the door and blocked it while Bayley hit him and punched him in the chest. Meeze took every blow until one of her hits smacked him in the face. Meeze grabbed her arms.

"Bayley, calm the fuck down and listen. For once, can you be a grown woman and fucking listen to what the fuck I have to say?" Meeze shouted. Bayley was tired and out of breath. She could feel her baby kicking, so she sat down on the floor to hear what Meeze had to say.

"Okay, I'm listening."

She looked up at him with much attitude. Meeze leaned back on the door and rubbed his face.

"That's the baby Lucky was pregnant with. It was too late for her to get an abortion..." Meeze paused, thinking she was going to flip out at the sound of Lucky's name, but she just looked up at him, waiting to hear the rest.

"Okay, keep going. It's Lucky's baby. I already knew it was too late for her to get an abortion, and what the fuck does that have to do with us? She can't keep her own baby?"

Meeze smacked his lips.

"It has a lot to do with you, because he is going to be a part of our lives. He's coming to live with us."

Bayley raised her left eyebrow.

"Our life? That's you and Lucky's baby. I don't want anything to do with anything that came out her raggedy pussy."

Bayley rolled her eyes. She couldn't stand Lucky and wanted to punch the bitch in the throat if she had the chance. Dragging her from the window wasn't enough, especially after she helped jump Amiah.

"Bayley, will you grow the fuck up, and stop sounding childish. Lucky is dead, so I have to keep my son. Now, if you can't respect that, then I'll go on my own way and take my son and my daughter. The bitch is fucking dead. She is dead so that I could secure our future and our family. You gon' help me with my lil' nigga and my daughter if you wanna continue to fuck with me, and, that's real..."

Bayley shook her head and chuckled. She couldn't be too mad, because the baby was conceived when she and Meeze weren't sure what they were doing. She was angry that she wasn't the first one to have his baby, but she had decided in her mind that she was going to take the baby in. She was extremely pissed at Meeze and was going to continue to be mad for a while.

"What's his name?" she asked with her same attitude.

"He's a junior."

There was a brief silence.

"Well, did you get a DNA test to at least be sure?"

"Yup. The results went to my mama's house. They are 99.999 percent."

Bayley shook her head. She couldn't see herself being selfish, seeing that Lucky was dead. She loved Meeze and was riding with him to the end... even if that meant having his son call her mommy.

"Nigga, you better be glad I'm pregnant and I like kids, because that baby would be at Martha's. Get him, and let's go. Miah has a cleanup crew. We can leave."

Bayley struggled to get up from the floor, and Meeze helped her up. He tried to reach in for a hug, but Bayley pushed him away.

"Nigga, don't touch me. I'm mad at your dog ass. We need to have a long talk, because I don't want any more secrets. You better apologize to my best friend. She doesn't want your punk ass friend anymore, so don't say that shit again."

"Ain't no other secrets, and yeah right. Amiah knows she misses that dick, but I'll apologize to her ass."

Meeze laughed and tried to hug Bayley again. Bayley pushed him away again.

"Yeah, whatever. Take me home, and I am not taking care of your baby tonight, but I'll help out since Mama Elaine is tired. I'll let you know when I am ready to have him full-time."

Meeze chuckled and walked off behind her. He was relieved that Bayley didn't take things to the extreme, because she could have left him and said fuck his son, but she didn't. Once again, she had proved her loyalty to Meeze, and that's why he loved her.

CHAPTER SEVEN

Pretty Bird

Bayley and Baby Girl sat in the quad of USC, waiting for Amiah to come out of class. They were all heading out to celebrate Baby Girl's new job. She had only been in school four months, and someone she met in class had hooked her up with an office assistant job at the local news station. She was finally going to work a real job, and it made her feel like a normal girl. She had dropped her stripper name, Baby Girl, and told everyone to call her Reeka.

"Damn, Miah always takes forever and a day to come out of class," Bayley said in an aggravated tone. She and her baby were hungry, and she hadn't eaten in two hours.

"Girl, you know she is probably somewhere being smothered by Braden's ass," Reeka joked, knowing Amiah was always with Braden.

"I'm sick of his ass. He doesn't even like us. I see that bullshit frown he makes when we come around. I was over Miah's house playing Spades with them, and he kept telling her to make me leave like he was fuckin', and she is not letting him hit that."

Reeka laughed.

"Oh, she ain't giving it up?"

"Hell nah. You know she is saving that pussy for Oxy, but she playin'."

"Well, you know Miah. She wants what she wants."

Reeka shook her head. She knew Bayley didn't want Amiah with Braden, because she wanted her to be with Oxy. Reeka was just happy to see Amiah happy, because Reeka still felt like Oxy was a jerk for cheating on Amiah.

"Her ass needs to want somebody else, because Braden, the bitch boy, is not it."

"Well, I think Miah looks cute with her new boo," she smiled. Bayley smacked her lips.

"Yeah, whatever you say, Reeka. You just hate Oxy too."

At that moment, Amiah, Braden, and Jonve hit the corner laughing, and talking.

"Look at him that's walking with Braden. I'm finna hook you up," Bayley said to Reeka. Reeka laughed.

"Hook me up? Whatever, girl. Don't none of these college niggas want my ass."

When it came to hooking up, outside of getting a guy to turn a trick, Reeka became shy, and her confidence level got low. She always looked at herself as damaged goods ever since the night her virginity was snatched away from her.

"Girl, bye. Your ass is bomb. Watch… his fine ass is going to be all over you."

Bayley thought Jonve would be a good catch for Reeka. At the party, she got to know him a little and saw his personality. He was nothing like Braden. Jonve was a football player but born and raised on the eastside of Los Angeles. All his family members were bloods, but he decided to take his life on a different path. He had no problem dating girls with flaws and girls with a little attitude.

"What's up, y'all? Y'all ready to go?" Amiah said with a smile on her face.

"Hell yeah, bitch. Your ass be taking forever to come out of class," Bayley said with much attitude as she and Reeka stood up from the bench. Braden frowned up his face.

"Why do you always have to be so ghetto with all of that cursing and being loud?" Braden said in disgust as if Bayley left a bad taste in his mouth.

"Nigga, because I can, and you got me fucked up. I'm not ghetto. You better get your friend, Miah!"

"Braden, you can't talk to my best friend like that. You are tripping right now," Amiah shot at him. She hated that Braden did not like Bayley, and she clearly knew Bayley was not feeling Braden.

"You are right. That's your friend, not mine, so I don't have to deal with that on a daily," Braden said to Amiah.

"Nigga, you better shut the fuck up while you can, before this turns into a serious issue."

Bayley was furious at Braden. This was their first argument, and she was ready to call Meeze and have him set Braden straight. Amiah pulled Braden away so that she could talk to him. She didn't like him and Bayley going back and forth, and she had to let him know. She also knew Bayley was quick to call Meeze, and it wasn't that serious.

"Well, anyway... what's up, Jonve?" Bayley said, putting her attention on Jonve. He looked her up and down, trying to remember her face. That's when it hit him.

"Oh, shit... Bayley? I see that nigga that dragged you out the party knocked you up," Jonve said in an excited tone. He had no hard feelings against Bayley or Meeze. He had just met her that night, so there was no need to be upset.

"Yup, he sure did, and we are engaged, but I want you to meet my other bestie, Reeka. She is new here at the school and looking for a friend," Bayley smirked. Jonve looked over at Reeka and immediately became attracted to her. She had her red hair pulled into a curly puff ball, and she was wearing a business suit. He thought her big brown eyes were dreamy, and her ass was fat.

"Well hello, Reeka?"

Jonve took her hand and kissed it softly.

"Well, I am going to wait for you and Miah in the car. You two can thank me later."

Bayley winked and walked off. She waddled off to the car. She did not want to go by Amiah and Braden while Reeka talked to Jonve.

"So, what's your name again?" Reeka asked, almost tongue tied. Jonve was sexy. He was tall, brown skinned, and his arm muscles were big in his practice jersey. Reeka had never been with a football player, so Bayley hooking her up with Jonve was a good look for her.

"My name is Jonve, but everybody just calls me Jon. So, you just started, huh? What is your major?" Jonve asked with a smile.

"My major is journalism. I'm trying to become a news reporter."

Reeka truly felt good not saying she was a full-time stripper. Jonve nodded his head.

"That's what's up, beauty, but I have to get to football practice. How about we exchange numbers, and we can finish this conversation over dinner?"

Reeka smiled.

"I'd like that."

The two exchanged numbers. Jonve and Braden then headed to practice.

"I see you are getting used to the college life," Amiah said with a smile.

"Yeah, a little... but this will be my first dinner date that didn't have money or sex involved, because my ass is going to be like you. I'mma take my time letting another nigga hit this good pussy."

Amiah laughed.

"You'll be fine. Trust me."

The girls then quickly walked to the car, because Bayley was calling both of their phones back to back...

***

Reeka walked through BR's club, heading to his office. She was so happy that she was finally telling him that she would no longer be dancing in his club. She thought she would be dancing and tricking forever, but she was now twenty-two and retiring. She walked through the club and looked at all the women shaking their ass for cash. She was so glad that wasn't her anymore. She couldn't wait to wrap up her meeting with BR and never step foot in there again. She knew her new job didn't pay her close to how much she was making in the club, but she was content with that. She had money stashed, and BR owed her one more check which was something he gave her every month, because she was bringing him so much money on her ten-hour shifts.

As she was passing the bar, her sister, Omeeka, was sitting at the bar with a trick hovering over her from behind. Omeeka spotted Reeka walking by and grabbed her by the arm to stop her.

"What's good, baby sis? Long time no see," Omeeka said with a smile.

"Hey, big sis. Shit, school has been keeping me busy, and I just got a job earlier today," Reeka said with a smile. She knew her sister would be proud of her because she always told her to go out in the world and live her life the way she was supposed to. Omeeka knew the life she lived wasn't for her sister ever since the night her mother forced her into prostitution.

"You mean school and hanging with your new friends? That's what's up about your job, though. Congratulations," Omeeka joked. She was truly proud of her sister and the moves she was making. She'd rather

her hang with some positive schoolgirls than the girls in the club.

"Yeah, that too, and thanks. I'm trying to change my life to the fullest. You know this shit ain't for me anymore."

Omeeka nodded.

"Honestly, sis… this shit was never for you. Just don't forget about me when you get big, baby sis. I will always love you."

She reached in for a hug. Reeka hugged her back.

"Facts, sis. You know I will never forget you, and I love you too. You talking like I'm moving away though. You know we can still kick it and drink. A bitch still does her thing on her alone time. I'm still smokin'."

"Okay, well let me get back to this nigga. Call me tomorrow so that I can come through, and we can talk some more."

Reeka agreed to call her, and she walked off. Reeka loved her sister, but they both were on different paths. Reeka understood that her sister would always be about that life, and it was nothing that could be done about it.

Reeka walked off and continued walking to BR's office. When she knocked, she waited for a few seconds, and then BR's personal bodyguard opened the door to let her in. He then closed it and locked it. When she walked in, she spotted BR sitting behind his desk, looking at his MacBook screen. Oxy was on the opposite side of his desk, rolling up weed.

Oxy turned around when he heard the door close. The both of them looked at Reeka. She had a different look about her. They were used to seeing her in club outfits or costumes, but she was dressed all the way down. She was wearing a pair of Michael Kors tennis shoes, some jeans, and a sweater. Her hair was in a bun with a pair of gold hoops in her ears, and she was carrying a black Birkin bag. Reeka wasn't expecting Oxy to be there, but she was kind of glad he was so that he could hear when she laid all her accomplishments on BR. She still held it on her heart that Oxy said she was pretty much a bad bitch with no goals, but she was ready to prove him wrong.

"What's up, BR? What's up, Oxy?" Reeka said as she sat in the chair in front of BR's desk that was next to Oxy.

"What's up, Baby Girl?" Oxy said and nodded his head.

"Yeah… what's up, Baby Girl? What brings you into my office after not coming in to work for two weeks and not calling me?" BR said. It wasn't that she wasn't coming in. He was more concerned about her. It was unusual for her to not show up to work and not call him to let him know what was going on with her.

"About that… Well, first… I don't go by Baby Girl anymore. I go by my government name now, Reeka Lovell."

BR and Oxy laughed.

"Okay, Miss Reeka… so are you going to tell a nigga why you haven't been at work?" BR asked as he stroked his chin hairs.

"I checked into USC about four months ago to take up journalism, and it has been taking up all my time."

Oxy gasped.

"What? Baby Girl… I mean… Reeka is in school? That's what's up!"

"Yeah, that's a good look for you. I always saw you as one of the girls to go and do something with your life. You are a woman, and a beautiful black Queen. Long as you use your brain, you can do whatever you want."

BR spoke to her with respect and encouraged her all the time. Out of all the girls in his club, he looked at Reeka differently... kind of like a little sister. She was young, and he knew her backstory, so he always treated her good.

Oxy passed Reeka his blunt. She took a long pull and then let out the remainder of the smoke.

"Thank you for always blessing me with your kind words, BR. The only thing I am going to miss about this place is you," she smiled.

"So, you leaving too... damn. You were one of my money makers. How are you going to get money now? School is expensive," BR asked. Reeka passed the blunt to BR to keep it in rotation.

"I got a job today at Channel 11 News as an office worker."

Oxy fell out his seat like he was so shocked to hear Reeka's life changes. Reeka laughed.

"Boy, get up. You are so dang childish! Yes, I got a job, so I will be living off my checks and the money I saved up working for you. They pay me thirteen dollars an hour for seven hours a day... four days a week, so I'll be okay. I just want to live a normal life. You feel me?"

"Yeah, I feel you."

BR reached into his desk drawer and pulled out a wad of bills. He then put the money in his money counter and counted out ten thousand dollars.

"Well, here is your last pay. If shit ever goes bad, you know you can always come back and work for me, but let's hope that never happens."

Reeka took the money and stuffed it in her purse.

"Thank you, BR. It's all love."

She stood up.

"Damn, Reeka. I'm impressed. Well, can a nigga take you to dinner or something to celebrate your accomplishments... not on no sex shit... just as friends?"

Oxy smiled.

"No, thanks. I have a date tonight with my new college boo. Plus... my bestie, Amiah, wouldn't even approve that. Besties over ex's," Reeka said and laughed as she started walking over to the door.

"You have truly killed me tonight, Reeka. Tell Amiah I said what's up, though," Oxy added with a smirk.

"Now you know I'm not doing that. Bye, guys. I'll see y'all around."

BR instructed his bodyguard to walk Reeka to her car, because she had all that cash on her. Reeka walked out the door feeling good. She had finally closed that horrible chapter in her life with stripping and prostitution, and she was never turning back.

CHAPTER EIGHT

Life Changing Part 2

*M*eeze and Bayley sat at a table in his restaurant that was still under construction while Oxy's lawyer, Araceli, went over all the necessary paperwork to finalize the ownership of his restaurant. Meeze was so geeked to be stepping away from the street life and becoming a family man with Bayley and his kids. Bayley was due any day, and his son was getting bigger by the day. They were constantly giving away clothes and buying new ones, because he was getting so long, and he was chubby.

"N'mere, I don't know how many times I am going to say that I am so proud of you," Bayley said as she had N'mere, Jr. on her lap, bouncing him on her knee so he wouldn't start up his usual crying.

Bayley had fallen so in love with N'mere, Jr., like she had birthed him herself. Even though taking care of a baby and getting ready to birth another one was hard at the age of nineteen, she managed it all with still going to school and working on her degree. She had everyone around her to help her out, so she was able to take a load off whenever things got overwhelming for her or when she needed to go to school.

After she broke the news to Reeka and Amiah, they weren't shocked that N'mere had a baby with Lucky. They were just shocked that Bayley had stepped up to the plate and was keeping her cool about the situation, even saying she wanted to legally be his mother by adopting him in the future. The girls were so happy that she had stepped up and become a real woman for N'mere. They both fell in love with N'mere, Jr., calling him their nephew.

"This soul food restaurant is going to be the hottest thing going since M&M's soul food restaurant. You two are going to make plenty of money," Araceli said as she slid more paperwork to Meeze.

"That's good, because this is his dream. As long as this business makes him some money, he will stay out the streets, so I am truly looking forward to this place opening soon."

Meeze laughed.

"Yeah, this restaurant will change all the lives around me, especially mine."

Meeze slid all the papers back to her.

"Well, I'll have this place open for you in no time. All you have to do is do the hiring. I'll take care of everything else."

Meeze nodded.

"My lady here will take care of all the hiring."

Meeze was on the road of success. He had his woman, his kids, and his new place of business. He even checked himself into culinary school so that he could join his line of professional chefs he already had lined up for interviews. He wanted to take a few of his home boys from being underground chefs and put them in his kitchen. He looked over at Bayley, and she had gone from looking happy to having a bitter look on her face. She was rubbing her stomach and rocking N'mere, Jr. to sleep.

"What's wrong, babe? You good?" Meeze said in a worried tone.

"Yeah, you don't look so good, mama. I am going to wrap this meeting up now for you guys," Araceli said, noticing Bayley's face.

"I think I am having contractions," Bayley said and handed N'mere, Jr. to Meeze. As soon as Bayley stood up, it started to look as if she had wet her pants. Bayley held her stomach and slouched over. That's when she felt the warm amniotic fluid going down her thighs in her sweats.

"Oh, shit," Meeze said when he noticed Bayley's wet sweats.

"Oh my God, mija. N'mere, you have to get her to a hospital," Araceli said and stood up. She grabbed the baby from Meeze so that he could help Bayley to the car. She was in so much pain that she couldn't say a word. She started crying while holding her stomach. Meeze picked her up with all his strength and carried her to the car. He secured Bayley in the front seat and then put N'mere, Jr. in his car seat. He then hurried straight to the hospital so that Bayley could finally deliver their daughter... baby Cassidy.

CHAPTER NINE

"*Good morning. My name is Laura Chang,*" the female newscaster said with a serious look on her face.

"*I'm reporting live from the Los Angeles River where two bodies were found in the water two days ago. A tourist saw a black body bag floating and called the police. The women have been identified as Prisetta James, age twenty-nine, and Ashley Wright, age twenty-four. Police are looking for anyone that knows anything about what happened to these two women. If you have any information, please call your local police station. Back to you, John.*"

The camera went back to the studio.

"*It's really sad how someone could do those poor women like that,*" the newscaster said.

Amiah sat in a nearby coffee shop, waiting on Braden to arrive so they could go to the gym. As she sat and sipped her steaming hot green tea, she looked up at the TV over her head that was playing the news. She shook her head as they showed Lucky and Pricey's face on the news for someone to come forward with information on the killer. She knew exactly who killed them, but she wasn't telling anyone anything, but that just confirmed her suspicions of Oxy being on a rampage. They weren't even together, and he was keeping his promise to make Lucky and Pricey pay for what they did, even though it had been a year.

Although Amiah and Braden were spending a lot of time together, she still thought about Oxy from time to time. Times when she was at home studying alone, she thought of him, wondering what he was doing or who he was with. She hadn't had sex with Braden yet, but she knew Oxy was out doing his thing. She vowed she wouldn't call him, even when she thought about him when she was horny. She and Braden fooled around, but there was nothing like Oxy's touch, and she hated that.

Amiah was snapped out of her thoughts when she felt someone touch her shoulder.

"Hey, pretty lady. Good morning."

Amiah snapped out her thoughts when she heard Braden talking over her shoulder. She looked up at him and smiled. Although she and Braden bumped heads on a few things, especially when it came to dealing with Bayley, Amiah still liked him. He was always a fresh breath of air for her in their alone time, and he catered to her every need.

However, Oxy was almost impossible to be *a thing of the past* for her, because something always reminded her of him, especially with the news constantly playing her brother's death and the death of Pricey and Lucky. She figured since he had stopped bugging her and sending her flowers to her class since he could no longer send them to her dorm, he had forgotten all about her and moved on to another girl. She was just going to move on and hope for the best for him in his life.

"Good morning, Braden. It took you long enough. You always have me waiting in the mornings when you know that I like to work out and then get to class on time," Amiah said with a slight attitude. Braden was always late, and she hated it.

"I'm sorry. That nigga, Jonve, had my house keys, so I couldn't lock up my apartment, but I see you are watching the news. That's messed up about what happened to those girls. I hope they find that creep and lock him up. I feel like no one deserves to die," Braden said with disgust. It was all over everywhere about Pricey and Lucky's bodies being found by the LA River in one body bag. Amiah turned up her nose at Braden.

"Well, before you call the killer a creep, let's get the whole story about what the so-called victims did. You are always so quick to judge," Amiah said, low-key taking up for Oxy. Yes, she had no business secretly taking up for him, but the little feelings she had left for him made her very defensive of Oxy. She knew he always had a reason to kill and would never kill anyone unless they betrayed him or there was money involved. Oxy had told her so many stories in the past about his reckless street life, and it stuck with her all the time. She wasn't scared of anything he had done, because she knew he would never hurt her physically, no matter how mad he was at her.

"Okay, Miah… I didn't know you cared that much about a killer's feelings. If somebody ever made me that mad though… I wouldn't kill them. I'd just let the law handle it. That's what it is for, right?"

Braden raised his eyebrow.

"Well, that's the difference between you and a killer…"

She paused, almost saying too much. Sometimes, Braden's square ways annoyed her. Yes, Amiah was a schoolgirl, but she understood hood nigga shit... something Braden knew nothing about.

"Well, anyway... are you ready to hit the gym. After that huge plate of cheese fries last night, I feel like a fat nigga."

Amiah laughed. "Yeah, all that grease on those fries... I'm surprised you didn't wake up with chest pains."

Braden laughed.

"Whatever, health freak. Let's get out of here."

Amiah had no shame in being cautious of what she put in her body. She loved junk food, but she knew she had to eat clean and take care of herself as she got older. After her mother died, her doctors put her as a high-risk patient for cancer. She did not want to be diagnosed with anything that was going to take away part of her life, so she decided to continue with the diet she and her mother were on.

Amiah stood up, Braden grabbed her gym bag and put his arm around her as they made their way through the coffee shop and out the door. For the rest of that morning, and for the first time in a long time, she had Oxy on the brain, even considering calling him, but she made up her mind that she wasn't and went on about her day with school, and Braden.

***

As Amiah was running on the treadmill, listening to her new song she had recorded a couple of days prior, her phone started ringing in her headset. She looked at the caller ID, and it was Bayley. She smiled and then answered.

"What's up, bestie? How are you and my babies?" Amiah asked.

"Miah, Bay is having Cassidy right now. You gotta come to the hospital. Her water broke at my restaurant," Meeze said with urgency. She could hear Bayley moaning and yelling from pain in the background. Amiah stopped the treadmill and got off.

"Damn, I have class in about thirty minutes, and I have a damn test. Tell her I will be there as soon as I can. How is she and the baby doing?"

Amiah walked into the locker room so that she could shower, head to class, and then head to the hospital. She was so excited to meet her god baby, but this test was going to either make her or break her, so she had to go to class.

"The doctor said she has about another hour before she delivers. She is eight and a half centimeters, so head to class and come up here, ASAP."

Amiah agreed and hung up her phone. She quickly went to find Braden so they could head to the school. She knew she had to get to Bayley, ASAP. She wanted to be there when the baby was being born, but she knew school was going to make her miss it all.

When she found Braden, he was near the weights. After waiting for him to finish his last lifts, they finally left. Amiah got to the school in record time. She went and took her test, which took two hours, and ditched Braden when she left her class. She didn't want him coming to the hospital with her, messing up Bayley's special moment. Plus, Meeze was going to be there. She knew with Meeze being around, if Braden started talking crazy to Bayley, things would escalate quickly. She was making sure she avoided all of that.

She pulled into the hospital and exited the car. She rushed inside and got her visiting pass. As she was walking the hall to the elevator, she spotted Meeze and Oxy in the cafeteria, talking. Her heart fluttered seeing Oxy's face, but she kept walking. She wanted to get to her best friend more than anything.

She got on the elevator and headed straight to Bayley's room. Before she walked in, the nurse asked Amiah to wash her hands. After she washed her hands, she walked into Bayley's room. She and the baby were sleeping. The baby was in a small plastic bassinet next to Bayley. Amiah walked over to the bassinet and looked inside.

"Awww," Amiah said in a soft tone when she laid her eyes on Bayley's baby girl. Her skin was light, and she was so tiny. She was swaddled in a baby blanket with a pink headband on her head. Amiah stroked her tiny head, rubbing her silky hair. Amiah wanted a baby of her own, but she wanted to wait until she was ready. She had so much going on in her life that she felt like a baby would stop her in her tracks. She thought Bayley was strong for being able to handle school with now having two kids and wanting to continue to graduate on time. Amiah felt like she didn't have that kind of strength nor the man like Bayley had. Braden didn't even want kids until he was in his late thirties, and Amiah didn't want to wait that long. She knew for a fact that she and Oxy were pretty much done. She knew he wanted kids, but he probably didn't want them with her anymore.

"Isn't she beautiful?" Bayley said, snatching Amiah out her thoughts.

"She's a doll, best friend. I am so proud of the woman you are becoming. I am so happy for you and N'mere."

Bayley smiled.

"Thank you, best friend. I know all of this is going to be challenging for me, but I have my family and my man, so I know I got this."

Bayley reached over and took her baby from the bassinet. She was so in love.

"I can't wait to have a baby of my own, but it's not my time yet."

"It will be... once you give Brandon a chance again and stop fooling around with Braden's ass."

Bayley started brushing her baby's hair.

"Speaking of him, I just saw him in the cafeteria with N'mere. Has he been up here yet?" Amiah asked. She did miss Oxy, but she honestly didn't know where they stood since it had been so long. She was also so used to being with Braden, that she often forgot about her feelings for him.

"Yeah, he was up here. You know he doesn't have a girl and hasn't been fucking with any bitches. You know N'mere will tell me anything I want to know when he has been drinking."

Amiah laughed lightly, not wanting to make the baby cry.

"You really want me with him... huh, best friend?" Amiah said.

"Yes. You two were just in a bad place at the time, so shit happened. I really, truly think you two are made for each other."

She smiled and handed the baby to Miah. Miah cradled the baby into her arm.

"Between me and you, bestie… I still love him, but I just don't know. I'm with Braden now. I can't just leave him and try and pursue Brandon. I don't even know if I'm ready to take that route again. What if he hurts me again?"

"You think a football player isn't going to eventually start having wandering eyes… especially with him going off to the pros and you not giving him none? Trust me… those football niggas cheat more than hood niggas, and they love white women."

Amiah laughed.

"Best friend, you are crazy, but, I don't know. I'll eventually try and break it off with Braden to see what's up with Brandon, but not right now."

Amiah couldn't believe that she was considering getting back with Oxy, but there was no denying it anymore. After seeing Bayley with her little family, she wanted that too. She knew she could secure that with Oxy, and she wanted to go for it, eventually.

"Well, don't wait too long, because you know all the girls want Oxy. He is a big deal in these streets right now. I heard he was a millionaire too."

Bayley reached for her baby so that she could try and breastfeed her.

"Don't forget, I am a millionaire my damn self. I don't want his money. I want his love and his loyalty."

Bayley nodded her head.

"That's why I love you… always on your boss shit."

"Well, I am going to get out of here before Braden starts calling me. I left him at the school, and he doesn't have his car. I drove."

"Okay, best friend. Come back tomorrow, but the doctor said I should be out of here before the week is over."

Amiah snapped a few pictures of the baby and sent them to Reeka. She hugged Bayley and left the hospital to go get Braden.

***

Company...

Amiah and Braden were at his house chilling. The two of them had been going hard with everything they had going on in their lives, so they just wanted to chill and watch movies. Amiah was cool with that since she was just getting over a cold and still had no time to rest her body. It was also her cheat night from her diet, so pizza, popcorn, and snacks were on the menu for them.

"So, me and my boys are getting a VIP section at Club LUX tomorrow night, and I wanted you to come with me," Braden said to Amiah as he put a slice of pizza on his plate.

"I don't know, Braden. I've just been chilling. I am not really trying to hit the scene," Amiah said in an uninterested tone. She wasn't a party girl, at all. Besides school and working on her businesses, all she wanted to do was use her days off as chill days.

"Come on. It will be fun. We can dance and have a good time. It's a nineties party. I heard Reeka was coming with Jonve," he said, knowing if she heard her friend was coming that she would go. Amiah thought about it. She really wasn't in the mood, but since Reeka was going, she decided to give in.

"Okay, I'll go if Reeka confirms that she is going for sure."

"Oh, she is going. She and Jon have been together ever since that night they went out."

After sending Reeka a text. Reeka confirmed that she was going, so Amiah told Braden she was going. Braden was so happy that she agreed, because he wanted the hottest girl on his arm when he stepped in the club. After they ate their pizza, Braden then turned off the lights and cuddled up with Amiah on the couch to watch their movie. Thirty minutes into the movie, Braden had his hand in Amiah's shirt, doing his usual fondling to her nipples.

Amiah rested her head on his chest as he played with them, making her wet. He then slid his other hand into her panties, because all she was wearing was a black tank top and silk boy shorts. Braden started rubbing her clit in a circle, making her wetter. Amiah let out a light moan from his touch. She was so horny that she was ready to finally take it to the next level with Braden. Amiah turned around to face him. She kissed him on the lips, and then their tongues tied, making Braden's dick rise. Amiah felt his dick poking her. She knew he wanted her, and for the first time, she wanted him too.

Braden sat up, and Amiah laid on the couch. He climbed on top of her and started grinding his pelvis on her while he was in between her legs, dry humping her. He started kissing her neck while Amiah was grinding on him from underneath. Her silk panties were soaked.

Amiah started sliding his sweats down. Braden became excited. He could feel his heart racing as Amiah slid his sweats down and grabbed his six inches of dick. Braden wasn't even close to as big as Oxy was, but Amiah was going to make the most of it.

"I want you to go down on me," Amiah said in a begging tone. It had been so long since she had some head, and she wanted to feel Braden's tongue. Braden slid down and sucked on her titties. Then, he made his way down to her clit. He took the tip of his tongue and started licking her clit. As Braden continued to lick her with the tip of his tongue, she realized he didn't even know how to eat pussy. He wasn't putting his face in it like Oxy and Derrick used to do, and that annoyed her. She tried to push his face into her pussy, but he locked up.

"Okay, that's enough. I want to feel you," Braden said as he came up from in between her legs. Amiah was truly disappointed in his head game, but she was still so horny, so she was ready to feel him too, hoping he was better in the stroke department. Braden picked Amiah up from the couch and carried her into the room as they kissed. He walked into his room and laid her on the bed. He walked over to his dresser and slid on a Trojan condom and walked over to the bed.

He parted Amiah's legs and slid one of his fingers in. She was still wet. He got on top of her and slid into her slowly. Braden started stroking her slowly, but his adrenaline started to take over. He started pumping her fast as he laid on top of her, sweating like he was putting in work. He was groaning and making Amiah extremely uncomfortable while he laid his dead weight on her. She was used to foreplay that led to a good dick down session, and this was not it. Two minutes later,

Braden was coming. He laid all his deadweight on top of her again and had the nerve to fall asleep on top of her.

"Braden, get your heavy ass up. You are squashing me," Amiah said as she tried to get Braden off her. Braden woke up and stood up from the bed.

"My bad. Let's go take a shower and finish watching the movie."

He walked off. Amiah stood up from the bed. She did not want to take a shower with him. She slid back on her panties and headed to the kitchen for some wine. She was truly disappointed in Braden's sex game, and now... she had to find a way to break the news to him.

CHAPTER TEN

Dirty Dancing

Amiah stood in her full-length mirror on her closet doors and checked out her appearance next to Reeka. They both were looking fly. There was a 90's party going on at the club they were heading to, and Amiah and Reeka wanted to follow the dress code. They wanted to go for the nineties rich girl look and nailed it. Amiah was wearing a white fur coat with a black mini dress, white Louboutin's heels, a pair of bamboo earrings, and a gold chain. Reeka was wearing the same thing, but she was wearing a leopard fur coat and leopard Louboutin stilettos.

"Jonve said this party is supposed to be live. It's some nigga's birthday that he knew from high school. But he didn't tell me his name."

"Well, it doesn't matter whose party it is. I just want to go have a good time with you and have a drink, but girl... let me tell you something, but don't tell Bayley. I don't want her to clown me," Amiah said as she slid on her white fur coat.

"Girl, what. Please don't tell me you are pregnant by Braden," Reeka said in a suspicious tone.

"Girl, hell no, and thank God. We finally had sex last night, and it was so wack."

Amiah shook her head. Reeka gasped, and then she laughed.

"Shut the front door. Bitch, what you mean it was wack?"

"Girl, the nigga nutted in two minutes, and his head game was sorry. He didn't even blame it on not getting pussy. He just collapsed his sweaty ass on me and fell asleep."

Reeka chuckled and shook her head.

"Damn, what a waste of a specimen. Maybe I need to give Jonve some before I become disappointed… so now what?" Reeka asked.

"Girl, I don't know, but I've been thinking about Oxy lately. I have to break up with Braden, and it isn't going to be easy. I think Braden loves me, but he hasn't said it yet. He talks about marriage and a house when he gets drafted, but I haven't been feeling it, especially since he's talking about playing for an east coast team and relocating."

"I know you love that nigga, Oxy, to death, and ain't nothing wrong with it. If you feel like he is the one for you, then try your hand again with him, but make sure you are sure and not just blinded by bad dick."

"You are right, Reeka. I'm still giving it some thought, but let's head to the club. Braden and them said they would be waiting for us out front."

The girls did their last touches and headed out the door to Amiah's Jag.

***

When they pulled up to the club, the line was packed, and the valet line was long as well, so they had to sit and wait their turn. There was no way they were going to be searching for parking and walking back to the club. As they were waiting for a valet driver to approach her car, she glanced at the royal blue Audi Q8 truck that was parked in front of the club.

"Oh wow... is that Oxy's truck?" Amiah asked Reeka. Reeka looked out the window.

"Girl, I don't know. That nigga be in so many cars and trucks. I can't even tell, but it might be."

"That looks like his main whip. I hope it isn't, because I am not trying to run into him with Braden on my ass."

Reeka laughed.

"Yeah, that would turn out pretty bad."

The valet driver finally came and tapped on the window. Amiah got out and handed him her push-to-start key. As soon as Amiah and Reeka stepped on the sidewalk in front of the club, all eyes were on them. Females were whispering, and men were whistling, but the girls paid them no mind and walked over to Braden and his crew.

"Damn, baby... you looking sexy as fuck," Jonve said as he wrapped his arm around Reeka. She blushed. Jonve complimented her no matter how she looked, and she loved it. He had been her boy toy for the past couple of weeks, and she was cool with that. He was making her feel like a woman more and more every day.

"Thanks, boo. You looking good yourself. I'm feeling this getup," Reeka said, referring to his outfit. He was wearing a pair of black jeans, some black Jordan 12s, and red, green, and black Cross Colours jacket from the 90's.

"What's up, Miah? You real distant," Braden said as he walked over to Miah and put his arm around her. After seeing that truck in front of the club, she was ready to get inside and be low-key just in case Oxy was in there. She didn't want him to see her with Braden and think she had completely moved on, because she hadn't.

"I'm good. I'm just ready to get inside so that I can get a glass of champagne or two to warm up. It's cold out here."

Braden shrugged his shoulders.

"Well, let's pull this money together so we can get in," Braden said, shaking off Amiah's unusual distance. He kind of figured she was just mad about the night before, but that was just how his sex game was. He didn't like giving head, and he always just wanted his nut. He thought since Amiah liked him and made him wait so long, she would be content with it, because it wasn't changing. He was a proud one minute man and never had a girl speak on it. Girls thought that he was so sexy that they didn't care about him lacking in the dick department.

Braden and his friends got their two thousand dollars together and handed it to the bouncer. He handed them their passes and had a waitress escorted them to the table. Amiah glanced around the club as they walked through, looking for any sign of Oxy, and she saw none. She didn't see any of his friends wandering around, nor did she see him at any of the VIP tables. That was a good sign, because she knew Oxy was low-key and kept his shit exclusive, so not seeing him at any VIP tables was a relief.

Amiah, Reeka, and Braden's crew stepped into the plush VIP section and sat down. As soon as the waitress brought all their bottles, they got the party started as the DJ played back to back nineties music. Everyone was drinking and having a good time, while more of their football and school friends started showing up in the section. The club had hit capacity, so the whole club started jumping.

Reeka and Amiah were feeling themselves as they danced in the VIP section with each other, Snapchatting and Instagramming. It had been a long time since the two of them had gone out and looked fly, and they knew they weren't going to be doing this again for a long time. They had school, work, and were helping Bayley with the babies, so they made their memories of their night out.

"Bitch, you look so fucking sexy. If that nigga, Oxy, is in here… when he sees you, he is going to be all over you," Reeka said with a huge smile on her face.

"Girl, I am not trying to see him tonight. As a matter of fact, let me put my shades on so I can disguise myself," Amiah said, sliding her shades out of her pocketbook and putting them on. Reeka laughed.

"Girl, your ass is crazy. I am about to get Jon and take him on the dance floor. His ass might get some tonight. He's looking bomb, and I'm drunk as fuck!" Reeka said with excitement. Her and Jonve were getting extremely close. She had already told him her background and her goals, and he respected everything about her. Reeka figured this night would be the night, for sure.

Amiah laughed.

"Okay… well, I'm going to take Braden out this VIP too. Look at him over there looking like a sad dog. He is too fine to have weak sex game… damn."

Amiah shook her head. They laughed. Amiah was tipsy, and she didn't want to ruin her night thinking about Braden's weak sex game. If she was going to be stuck with Braden for a while, she figured she might as well take charge and enjoy it.

Amiah walked over to Braden and stood in front of him. He was looking sexy in his nineties outfit. He was wearing an old-school, Adidas sweat jacket with a matching pair of Adidas tennis shoes. He had his hair cut in a fade with the Nas line in the front. Braden looked up from his bottle of champagne and spotted Amiah in front of him. He gazed at her with his hazel-green eyes with pity.

"What's up, superstar? I see you are having more fun with Reeka instead of me," Braden said in a sad and bitter tone. Amiah smiled, ignoring his pity. She had no interest in it, because her spirits were up, and she had liquor running through her bloodstream.

"Stop being bitter, Braden, and get up. Let's go dance," Amiah said as she pulled his arm to stand up. Braden stood up, and Amiah led him out to the dance floor near the DJ booth. She started grinding her ass on Braden as "If You Love Me" by Brownstone blared through the club. They were having a slow song session, and Amiah was taking advantage…

You will not hurt my pride, if right now you decide that you are not ready to settle down. But if you want my heart, then it's time that you start, to act like you're mine in the light and the dark.

If you love me, say it!

If you trust me, do it!

If you want me, show it!

If you need me, prove it!

Braden was loving every minute and feeling like he had the finest girl in the club dancing on him while people were watching them. Braden had his hand up Amiah's mini skirt, grabbing on her toned thighs, and kissing on her as much as he could. Amiah winded down low and then slowly brought her body up. She was feeling every word to the song. She was also feeling sexy and free. At that moment, the DJ switched up the music and started remixing a Migo's song.

"Yo, yo, yo! It's ya boy, DJ Gucci. I hope y'all are enjoying this nineties atmosphere we got going here tonight, but it's almost midnight, and I want to change it up for my gangsta niggas in here tonight. We got the birthday homie chilling up in the skybox tonight, looking over all y'all niggas having a good time at his birthday party. Ladies, let me hear y'all sing my young... fly... nigga..., Oxy, happy birthday right now! Oh yeah... shout out to all the Taurus' out there! Now, sing!" the DJ shouted over the microphone. On que, every woman in the club began to sing him *happy birthday.*

Amiah felt like she was going to faint when she heard the DJ say it was Oxy's birthday. She pulled her phone from her inside pocket of her jacket and looked at the date. Sure enough, it was Sunday, April 24th. All the thinking she had done about him in the last twenty-four hours, and his birthday did not cross her mind. She was so caught up in Braden with his weak sex game and her thoughts on how she was going to break things off, that she had forgotten about his twenty-fourth birthday. She knew for a fact he had saw her with Braden, now that she knew he was partying in the skybox of the club right over her. She should have known better, but this was her first time at this club, so she didn't even know or think about them having an exclusive VIP section looking over the club.

"I'll be back, Braden. I have to use the restroom," Amiah said as she began to walk off.

"Alright, I'll be right behind you. I have to go as well."

Amiah went into the restroom and paced.

Shit, shit, shit!

She walked into the stall and flopped on the toilet. She knew her next move was to get Reeka and get the fuck out the club before Oxy approached her without a care in the world, and she was with Braden. Then, she thought about going up to his skybox and telling him happy birthday before he made his way down. She didn't know what she was going to do once she ran into him at the end of the night, because she knew Braden wasn't going to want her to leave early if she told him she was leaving. Her car was with valet, and his was parked right out front. She knew they were going to bump heads while she was in front of Braden, and that made her nervous. She didn't want to end things on bad terms with Braden, because she cared about his feelings and had never told him about Oxy. She left him out for a reason. She wanted to protect him, just in case any of his demons ever came out in front of Braden.

At that moment, Amiah decided to get Reeka and leave. Braden was just going to have to be upset that she ditched him. She was just going to call Oxy later that night, wish him a happy birthday, and then see where their conversation went from there. She wanted to play it safe.

Amiah used the restroom, washed her hands, and then fixed her makeup. She then proceeded to open the door to find Reeka.

CHAPTER ELEVEN

Mercy

Oxy sat in the skybox of the hottest nightclub in Hollywood, over his limit with drinking. It was his 24th birthday, and Amiah was in the crowd, dancing on another guy. It made him so angry that she had moved on and didn't even notice whose party she was at. *How could she forget my birthday*, he thought to himself as he watched Amiah drop it low on her new boyfriend. It was all over the city that his exclusive "90's Baby" party was going to be at LUX, and Amiah clearly didn't get the memo, because Oxy knew for a fact she wouldn't bring him to the party on purpose. Oxy played it cool though. He had everybody that was somebody in his skybox, partying and networking, and he had Elecia clinging onto his arm like he was going to disappear if she had let him go.

Oxy and Elecia had been messaging each other back and forth on Facebook for a couple of weeks. He invited her to be his date for his party and promised if everything went good at the end of the night, she could be his birthday cake. Of course, Elecia was with it, especially since Oxy sent her over everything he wanted her to wear to his party, making sure she matched his swag on his arm.

They both had on matching Versace attire. Elecia was wearing a short wrap around Versace print dress with a pair of gold Giuseppe Zanotti heels. Oxy was wearing a silk Versace button-down shirt that matched Elecia's tight fitting mini dress, with a pair of dark Versace shades with the gold lion on the side of them, and Versace tennis shoes. He also played it cool for his homies. They were having a good time and making business connections, so he didn't want to ruin the party by punching Amiah's new boyfriend in the face in front of everybody. Therefore, he chilled.

He followed her closely as his jealousy built up. The way the dude she was with was feeling up her skirt and grabbing her ass, Oxy knew the nigga was fucking Amiah, and he couldn't stand it. He frowned up his face the whole time. At that moment, the DJ started talking over the microphone and flashed a spotlight into the skybox. That's when every woman in the club, including Elecia, started singing happy birthday to him. Oxy pierced his eyes on Amiah. She was looking sexy, and that made him angry too. She was with another nigga, looking her best on his birthday. That didn't sit well with him at all.

"Babe, where are you going? The bartenders are bringing your cake," Elecia said as Oxy snatched his arm away from her when he saw Amiah walk off, looking as though she was heading to the restroom. The skybox wasn't too far from the DJ booth where Amiah was, so he could see her every move.

"I'll be back."

He handed her his shades and hurried off. Oxy walked down the stairs that lead to the club area. His homie and body guard, who was Big Cuzz's little brother, Lil' Cuzz, stopped him.

"What's up, bro? Where you rushing off to? You need me?" Lil' Cuzz asked with a mean mug.

"Nah… I'm good, bro. I'm about to holler at this girl real quick," Oxy said and walked off. Oxy walked through the crowd with a slight stagger while women were trying to stop him and say happy birthday like he was a superstar. Ever since he opened his studio to every rapper that had money for studio time, and with his shoe service booming, his name was buzzing from corporate offices to the streets. All the ladies knew him from his social media pages.

Before he made it to the bathroom area, he took one of his gold chains off and slid the engagement ring he had gotten for Amiah months ago on his pinky. Even though it had been months, Oxy hadn't given up on the woman he loved and obsessed about. He walked up to the bathroom door and tried to push it open but it was locked. He stood there with his foot on the door, waiting for it to open. A couple of minutes later, he heard the water running inside. Once that door opened, Oxy pushed it wide open, pushed Amiah back into the one-stall bathroom, and locked the door.

"Oh my God, Brandon! What are you doing?" Amiah said loudly with the look of shock on her face.

"So, you're fuckin' cornball niggas now, Miah? You fuckin' that nigga?" Oxy said in an aggressive tone. Seeing another man love on Amiah hurt him and angered him. He didn't want anyone touching her. He thought he had made that clear when any other man had touched her in the past. He pinned her arms up against the wall with one hand.

"Let me go, Brandon. You are hurting me!"

Amiah tried to break away from his hold, but her five-foot-four frame wasn't strong enough to break away.

"You fuckin' that nigga? You love that nigga?" Oxy asked her over and over. He could feel his heart breaking with every word, all over again... almost in tears. He never loved a woman so hard. His emotions were all over the place and started flooding his brain.

"Brandon, you are drunk. Please, just let me go. I am not fucking anyone," Amiah pleaded. She knew he was drunk and emotional. She didn't want to say anything to upset him anymore than he was already.

"You're lying."

Oxy started pulling up Amiah's tight skirt. Before she could say anything else, Oxy had two fingers in her creamy hole and his tongue down her throat. Tears flooded her face as Oxy kissed her neck and lips while fingering her slowly. She was crying, because his kisses and touch brought back too many memories...all the nights he held her when she was getting over her mother's death, all the patience he had for her when she made him wait while she finished out semesters of school, when she really didn't have to make him wait, all the I love yous, and all the love they made in his bed... Yes, she missed him, but she still wasn't sure if she could trust him with her heart again.

"You're mine, Amiah. You're mine," Oxy whispered in her ear with his deep baritone voice. Chills were forming all over her body, but she didn't speak a word to him. She just couldn't. The feeling from his long fingers made her feel like she was going to come all on his fingers and hand. That's when she felt Oxy slipping a ring on her ring finger.

"You're mine."

Oxy let her arms go and took his fingers out of her before she came. He could feel her breathing heavily, and she was starting to moan lightly. He stepped back and looked at her. Amiah slid to the floor with a face full of tears, still not saying a word. Her emotions were all over the place. Oxy reached into his pocket and tossed a room key to his hotel suite in Beverly Hills on the floor.

"If you love me, you'll meet me at my room when you get rid of that square nigga you got out there... tonight. You were made for me, not him. You ain't built for that square shit like you think you are. You are built for a gangsta nigga like me."

He walked out the bathroom, leaving Amiah with a mind full of thoughts and a palm full of tears.

***

When Oxy walked out of the bathroom, he saw the guy that Amiah was dancing with and frowned. Braden frowned back, but then saw where Oxy was coming from. He immediately became worried about Amiah and headed inside of the women's restroom to see was she okay. When he walked in, he saw Amiah on the floor crying.

"Miah, did he do something to you? Say something... did he hurt you?" Braden said in an angry tone while trying to get her to look at him, but she never looked up. She only sobbed in her lap.

Braden stormed out of the bathroom and caught up with Oxy. He shoved Oxy so hard in the back that he stumbled into a table, knocking over empty liquor bottles and glasses. Oxy caught his balance and turned around. He turned around and saw that it was Amiah's boyfriend.

"What the fuck did you do to my girl, punk? Did you rape her?" Braden shouted. Oxy walked up to him and punched him in the mouth so hard that his lip started to bleed. Braden tried to punch him back, but Oxy hit him twice in the face, knocking him to the floor. After Oxy knocked him to the floor, he lost it. He kneeled down and started punching Braden in the mouth repeatedly.

"Oh, shit. We need security over here. The birthday homie is fighting!" the DJ said over the microphone while everyone started trying to move out of the way. Amiah came running out of the bathroom when she heard the DJ say Oxy was fighting. She knew it had to be Braden. She slipped out of her heels and made her way through the crowd. That's when she saw Meeze pulling Oxy up by his shirt off Braden. At least fifteen niggas were surrounding them, making sure nothing happened to Oxy. Therefore, she couldn't get to him, so she rushed to Braden's side and tried to help him up while she called Reeka's phone to let her know it was Braden fighting and to tell Jonve. Meeze and the rest of Oxy's crew hovered over Oxy and walked him out front to his truck. Meeze got into the passenger seat. Oxy got into the driver's seat, and drove off.

"What the fuck happened, bro? You good?" Meeze asked as Oxy did seventy on a main street, trying to find a freeway. He was so angry. He just wanted to get the fuck away from the club.

"That was Miah's nigga. That nigga shoved me from the back, so I shattered his shit," Oxy said. He slowed down a little when he saw police parked on the side of the road.

"Damn, bro. You want to go back and fuck that nigga up some more?" Meeze asked.

"Nah, I'm good. That nigga a civilian. I know for a fact that nigga gon' find out who I am and press charges. I fucked that nigga's face off, bro."

Meeze shook his head.

"Damn, bro. You know your knockout game is strong. I know you ain't trying to go back on the club's block, but I need my whip. Bayley is blowing me up. She must have already heard what happened."

At that moment, Oxy's phone had started ringing too. It was Elecia. He wasn't in the mood to be bothered with her anymore. He wanted to go to his room and chill… and possibly see Miah. He knew she still had love for him by the way she was kissing him back in that bathroom, so he had to ditch Elecia and figure out what he was going to say to her later.

Oxy went back to the club and dropped Meeze off on the corner so that he could get his car and go home. The two gave each other pounds, and Meeze walked off. Oxy then did a U-Turn and headed to Beverly Hills to his penthouse suite he had rented out for the week.

Lessons...

Elecia walked full speed to Oxy's penthouse suite with her dress, heels, and Oxy's shades in hand. She had to take an Uber home so that she could change her clothes, get her car, and then to the hotel to give Oxy a piece of her mind. After she saw Oxy fighting from the skybox and then heard who he was fighting, she was .38 hot. It had gotten around fast that it was Amiah's boyfriend he beat up, and the footage was already floating on Instagram.

She was embarrassed, because she had all her friends in the club thinking they were a couple. Everyone saw them walk in together and head to the skybox holding hands, so Elecia thought for sure it was going to be a good night and possibly a future for them. Elecia banged on the door as hard as she could. She didn't know if he was in there or not, but if he wasn't, she was going to wait for his ass.

"Aye, what the fuck are you doing?" Oxy asked in an aggravated tone as soon as he opened his room door. He had a blunt dangling from his lips with 21 Savage blaring through his Bluetooth speakers he had brought to his room. He was continuing his birthday alone and didn't want to be bothered unless it was Amiah.

"Nigga, what the fuck you mean *what am I doing*? I'm coming to check your ass! How the fuck you leave me to go fight your ex's new boyfriend in front of everybody? It was all over the fucking club what you did. Do you know how stupid that made me look?"

She pushed Oxy to the side and barged into his room. She was hoping Amiah was in there so she could blow the scene on both of them. Oxy frowned and closed the door.

"Made you look stupid? How I made you look stupid? I was the one fighting," Oxy said with a curious look on his face.

"You left my side to go fight Amiah's new boyfriend! Are you not hearing me when I say everyone knows that? I thought you were over her!" she shouted. She took the heels and dress and tossed it in Oxy's face. Oxy walked over to his phone and paused his music. He wanted Elecia out of his room, but he kept his cool with her.

"First, you need to stop all that yelling before security comes up here thinking something is going on. Second, I never said I was over Amiah. I just said we were broken up. Now, you need to step, Elecia. I'm chillin' right now, and I'm not in the mood for no more bullshit."

Oxy walked over to the table and sat his blunt in the ashtray. Elecia was right behind him, giving him a piece of her mind.

"I swear... you are so arrogant and thoughtless. Who do you think you are? You think you can just do whatever you want to me because I liked you? You think I give a fuck about you buying me a outfit that I could buy myself? I don't give a fuck about none of that shit, Brandon. I wanted you. I wanted your heart, and you knew that!"

Elecia pushed Oxy's forehead with her index finger. Then, out the blue, tears started flooding her face. Oxy looked at her with no emotions. All he knew was that, he knew a crazy bitch when he saw one, and he wanted Elecia out of his room before shit got crazy between them.

"Don't put your hands on me, Elecia. You knew you were just my date for my party. We never talked about you having feelings for me. What the fuck do you want me to do?"

Elecia was stressing him out. He did not want to argue with her, because it wasn't going to get them anywhere.

"But we talked about sex! That's all you think I am, is just a fuck? I want you to be a fucking man and stop leading me on! I really thought this would be the night for us, but you want that bitch, Amiah. She doesn't want you, Brandon. She wants that nigga she was with. How about that, nigga? Does that make you mad that the bitch doesn't want you anymore?" Elecia said in a deranged tone, pressing her finger against his forehead again.

"You need to leave, Elecia. You are stepping over your boundaries with that bullshit you're talking, and your ass is trippin'. Whatever we had, it's done."

Oxy was trying to keep his cool, because he wasn't in the mood to snap on her. He still had liquor in his system, so he didn't want to put his hands on her. She was emotional over shit she had made up in her head.

"Done?"

Elecia started laughing like a crazy woman.

"I got your *done*, nigga!"

That's when she pulled a large kitchen knife from her purse. Oxy backed up as she walked toward him with the knife and an evil smile on her face.

"Nigga, I am about to teach you a lesson about fucking me over and embarrassing me. You messed with the wrong bitch's feelings."

Elecia started swinging her knife. He was on the verge of pulling his nine-millimeter from his waist and shooting her, but she wasn't worth it. He was trying to work on his anger issues and violent ways, and Elecia was trying to blow it for him like Braden did. He knew he could take the knife away from her without popping her. He grabbed her arm with the knife in it and twisted it to her back. He was not going to let her stab him and mess his night up more than it was. Elecia started screaming like he was killing her. Oxy walked her to the door with her arm still twisted behind her back.

"Let me go, you punk ass nigga. I hate you! I hate you so much!" Elecia shouted with tears still streaming her face. Oxy didn't care or say one word in response. He didn't have anything else to say to her crazy ass. One thing he didn't need, was another crazy girl in his life. He had gotten rid of Erica and Pricey, so he didn't need Elecia with her mental issues. Oxy took the knife out her hand and slammed the door in her face before she could barge back in. Oxy dropped the knife to floor and walked back into his room. Once again, he didn't know what he had gotten himself into. All he knew was that he was done entertaining females.

Oxy picked up Elecia's dress, shoes, his shades, and knife. He stuffed everything in his duffle bag and zipped it. He figured he would just get his ten thousand dollars back for the dress and shoes since she didn't want it. He had money, but not money to waste, so it was going back to the store ASAP.

"Shit, these fuckin' bitches is crazy," Oxy said as he lit his blunt and turned back on his music like Elecia was never even there, hoping for Amiah to arrive.

CHAPTER TWELVE

Sacrifices

Amiah sat at Braden's island while he iced his lip and nose. His face was so swollen and busted that Amiah knew, eventually, he would have to go to the hospital for stitches. He was missing one of his front teeth and a few at the bottom. Amiah felt bad that Braden had endured an ass whooping from Oxy because of her, but that was why she didn't want Oxy to see her with him. She was afraid of his actions.

"Braden, are you sure you don't want me to take you to the hospital? Your face looks extremely painful," Amiah said in a soft tone. She knew Braden was angry, but she was concerned about his wounds.

"I said I will be fine, Miah. So, who the fuck was that guy? Why won't you tell me his name?" Braden said in a frustrating tone.

"He's my ex, Braden. That's all you need to know. I am not telling you his name, so forget it," Amiah said with an attitude.

"Why? Is he threatening you and making you protect him… huh?"

"He is not making me do anything, Braden. It's just not my place to tell you his name. I didn't tell you to go fight him for me. I can take care of myself."

"Your fucking ex shattered my face, and you don't want to tell me his name? Are you still fucking with him or something? I was fighting with him over you. I thought he raped you, Amiah. Do you know how serious that is? You know what... I think you should leave. I am really not feeling you right now, and this relationship is clearly over. Tell your ghetto ass ex-boyfriend I am pressing charges, and I am suing him for medical bills. My mother is coming right now to take me to the hospital."

Braden walked out the kitchen and laid on his couch to rest his pounding head.

He did not want to continue his argument with Amiah, and he didn't want her in his presence anymore. After all he had been through for her in one night, she couldn't give him a name. He saw where her loyalty lied, and it wasn't with him. Therefore, there was no need for him to take things further with her.

"Over? Are you serious, Braden? I didn't tell you to go push him... You know what, fine. It is over. I've been done with your ass in my mind for a long time now, and after last night, I was really done with you... with your little dick ass. I'm out."

Amiah grabbed her pocketbook from his island and left, slamming the door. She was glad Braden broke things off, because that made things easy for her. Amiah started her car and went home.

When she got home, she sat on the couch and looked at the time. It was two in the morning, and she was mentally drained, but when she took everything out of her jacket pocket, she remembered she had Oxy's room key, and she was wearing his diamond engagement ring. She decided she would take a shower and head over there. She knew now was the time for them to fix their broken relationship. She was ready to get him back, but they had a lot to talk about. She was going to spare him the talk and tend to his needs since it was his birthday, but after the love making was over, she wanted answers. She was craving his touch and could still feel his lips all over her from the bathroom incident. The way he was kissing on her, she knew he still wanted her, and she now knew where they stood. She was just hoping he didn't think she sent Braden to fight him, because that was the main thing she was trying to avoid.

After Amiah got out of the shower, she packed her bag with enough clothes, because she knew Oxy was not going to let her just stay one night with him. She then slid on a pair of black tights and a black crop top. She slid on her fur burgundy Fenty Puma flip flops with her burgundy fur jacket and headed out the door. Amiah pulled into the Beverly Hills hotel and gave her car to the late-night valet. After getting jumped by Pricey and Lucky in a hotel parking lot, she never parked in a parking lot again. She always valet parked.

She walked into the lobby of the hotel and walked over to the elevator. As she rode the elevator to the top floor, she looked at herself in the mirrors that covered the elevator walls. She had developed a whole lot, mentally and physically, since the first time she met Oxy.

She reminisced on the first time she laid eyes on him. His eyes let her know that he was looking for someone to love him so that he could level out the dark side of his life, and she wanted to be the one to love him. She still was a little girl then, but she understood love and the affect it had on people. She just never thought he would cheat on her. She didn't know her distant ways would make him stray away, but she figured he had grown tired of always having to wait for her. Now, she was going to fit him in her busy schedule and be the girl he needed. She then weighed out the good and the bad about Oxy. Yes, he did cheat on her, but he was charming, a protector, and he loved and cared for everyone around him. She couldn't lie… his sex game was like magic. That was the main reason she was on that elevator, heading to the top floor to work things out.

The dinging sound of the elevator snapped her out of her thoughts. She stepped out of the elevator and walked down the hall to the last door on the left. She stuck the key card in the door and it silently opened. When she stepped into the room and closed the door, the cold air coming from the air conditioner brushed across her face. She dropped her bag and walked through the cold, dark room. She made her way through the living room area, and then made her way over to the bed. Oxy had the curtains open, letting in the lights that lit up Beverly Blvd. She walked over to the bed and saw him laid out, still in his club clothes. His shoes were off, his shirt was unbuttoned, and he still had on all his jewelry. Amiah ran her long pearl colored stiletto nails down his chest. He was looking so sexy. She couldn't wait to climb on top of him.

Oxy opened his eyes and looked over at Amiah. He almost thought he was dreaming when he laid eyes on her. Something about her face was different. She looked mature, and sexy.

"Happy birthday, Brandon. Sorry it took me so long," Amiah said with a smile. He smiled back.

"Thanks... I'm just glad you showed up."

Oxy sat up, trying to shake off his tiredness from his drunken slumber. Oxy sat up on the edge of the bed and checked her out. Her body had changed since the day he had first met her. He remembered her having B cup titties and a small ass. Her stomach was always flat but not as toned as it was now. Since she was almost nineteen years old, her titties had gotten two sizes bigger and so did her ass from being in the gym.

"Damn, Miah. You look great. What have you been doing?" Oxy asked in a raspy, sleepy tone. Amiah giggled, knowing he would notice her developments.

"Working out... aging... you know... You like?" she asked with a smile, while rubbing her hands down her small waist.

"I love it."

Oxy sat at the edge of the bed and started kissing her flat stomach while sliding down her tights. She wasn't wearing any panties, and that excited him. He knew what she wanted, and he was going to give it to her. He cuffed her ass in his hands and ran his tongue down her stomach line, licking the vulva of her kitty. Amiah was already enjoying his fourplay... something she had missed and craved. Amiah slid off her jacket and let it fall to the floor. She stepped out her tights, and that's when Oxy leaned back on his elbows. He smirked. He honestly didn't think his bathroom incident would actually get her back into his presence. He thought that since he shattered her boyfriend's face and hemmed her up in the bathroom, she wasn't going to come to his suite, but he was still hopeful, and it worked.

"Come here, babe."

Oxy wrapped his arms around her waist and pulled her close. Amiah sat on his lap and started kissing on his neck and his lips. Oxy laid back on the bed. He was hungry to taste Amiah, so he slid her body up to his face and started feasting on her pearl tongue. Amiah moaned loudly as Oxy tongue fucked her while she rotated her hips on his face. She was in a zone. Oxy could feel his dick rising inside of his black True Religion jeans. He was ready to dig inside of Amiah and give her a session that he knew for sure would make her stay if she was deciding to leave before sunrise.

Amiah climbed off his face and started unbuckling his jeans. She slid them down, along with his Versace boxer briefs, and started stroking his nine inches. She looked at it and contemplated on putting it in her mouth, and she had made up her mind. Before she knew it, she had half of his dick down her throat. Oxy was shocked that she went down on him, but he laid back and enjoyed it.

"Just know that you are the first guy I ever gave head to, and I want to keep it that way," Amiah said and then swirled her tongue around the tip of his dick. She knew giving head was a fifty-fifty thing in a relationship, so she decided to start practicing now. She knew she would eventually get better at it.

Oxy looked at her and smirked. He was glad she didn't learn how to suck dick from her last dude, and he was pleased that he was her first. Oxy laid back and let her do her thing. Amiah had finally came up for air and climbed on top of him. She guided him inside of her slowly, because it had been so long since she had all of him inside her. Oxy started stroking her slowly from underneath while he gripped her hips. Amiah rested her head on his chest as he gave her slow, deep strokes. She was almost in tears from the pleasure and pain, but she loved it.

"You miss me, babe? Do you love me?" Oxy asked in a sexy tone as he continued to stroke her slow.

"Yes… I missed you, Brandon. Yes, I love you so much," Amiah cried out. Oxy could feel her tears falling. He sped up his pace and started hitting spots she didn't even know she had. Amiah couldn't take it anymore, so she took control and started riding his dick. She could feel herself about to cum, but it was a different feeling. She was grinding her hips on his pelvis and bouncing on his dick while he played with her nipples. Before she knew it, she was squirting all over Oxy, making the bed so soaked. She thought she had peed on herself.

"Oh my God! What the fuck?"

Amiah stood from the bed, out of breath and in shock. She had never squirted before. Every time she had sex with Oxy in the past, he had her doing something different. Everything she knew, Oxy had taught her. Now, she knew her pussy could squirt. Oxy laughed.

"You squirted, babe. You good. Now, bend over. That ass is looking right."

Oxy got behind Amiah and bent her over the bed. He then slid inside her gushiness, and for the next couple of hours, Oxy was digging Amiah out until they both fell asleep.

CHAPTER THIRTEEN

All I Have

*A*miah sat at the table in Oxy's penthouse suite, next to the city view window, flipping through a magazine for cosmetics while Oxy slept the day away. It was already three in the afternoon, and she couldn't wait for him to finally wake up, so they could talk. She was looking forward to starting their relationship over, but she had a lot on her mind. Braden was clearly done with her after Oxy punched him in the face, and she didn't tell him his name, but she needed some clarity before she moved forward. She had her ring sitting on the table, because as soon as he said the wrong thing, she was leaving him and never turning back. Oxy opened his eyes and tried to adjust to the afternoon sunshine that was shining into the room. He sat up in bed and rubbed his eyes. When he looked around the room, he locked eyes with Amiah.

"Oh shit! What's up, babe? What time is it?"

He gave her a half of a smile.

"It's 3:30 in the afternoon. I bet you don't even remember anything that happened last night."

Amiah sipped her piping hot green tea. Oxy stood up from the bed, only wearing his boxer briefs and black Versace socks.

"I remember everything that happened last night," Oxy said in a nonchalant tone. He walked over to his duffle bag and grabbed a tank top and a pair of sweats.

"Come sit with me, Brandon. I want to talk to you," Amiah said. Oxy slipped on his tank top and sweats and walked over to the table where Amiah was sitting. When he sat down, he rubbed his knuckles. They were a little swollen from his fight with Braden. He reached for a napkin and scooped some ice from the ice bucket that was on the table. He then applied the ice in the napkin to his knuckles. He glanced over at Amiah's ring sitting in the middle of the table. He frowned.

"Why aren't you wearing your ring?"

Amiah closed her magazine and sighed.

"Because, Brandon... you barged in on me in the restroom last night, and you beat up my boyfriend. How do you know if I want to be with you after all of that bullshit you pulled last night? You could have killed him, and everyone would have been pointing the finger at me."

"Because if you didn't want to be with me, you wouldn't be here right now, Miah. So, what now... you're leaving me again without settling our issue, huh?"

Oxy gave her a look that would kill if it could. He could feel himself getting angry, because he knew they were going to argue, and Amiah was going to leave him again, but he wasn't playing that game with her anymore. He was going to do whatever he had to do to make things right with them for good.

"I should! He broke up with me and never wants to see me again. He even said he is going to press charges on you when he finds out your name, and he is going to sue you. Do you just want me so you can walk all over me like some doormat? Why do you want to be with me so bad, Brandon?"

"I fucking love you. That's why, and you know that."

"I don't fucking know that. You fucking cheated on me, and you expect me to just take you back? I don't think so. And then, you slide a ring on my finger and expect me to just get over what you did to me? You know what? I think you need more time to think about us."

Amiah stood up from the table and started gathering her things. For some reason, she just couldn't get through their argument. Her heart was telling her to stay and work it out, but her mind was telling her to leave and get away from Oxy as far as she could. She always went with her mind, because it seemed like her heart was always leading her into the wrong place. Oxy was furious that she was trying to leave, and he wasn't letting her walk out on him this time. He grabbed all her stuff and tossed it across the room.

"What the fuck is wrong with you, throwing my things?" Amiah shouted and tried to start picking up all her stuff. Oxy grabbed her by the arm.

"No, what the fuck is wrong with you, Miah? Do you fucking enjoy watching me be miserable over your silly ass?"

"No, but I just feel like you are not ready for us. You told me you would protect me and love me, but you let your ex jump me, and then you cheated on me!" she shouted. She had finally brought up the situation with Pricey. She had pushed it to the back of her mind. But with everything going on, she was ready to throw it in his face.

"I said I was sorry a million times, man andI handled that Pricey situation. I gave you your space. You came back to me, and now you are trying to leave me again? Stop fucking walking out on me, Miah! I already lost my mom and my son. I don't want to lose you, babe. Please, just stay!"

Oxy got on his knees, begging her to stay. He didn't care how soft it made him look by begging, but that was his last resort.

Amiah felt so sorry for him as she looked down at him and into his eyes. He had that same look in his eyes when he first told her he loved her. She started having a change of heart about leaving. She just couldn't leave him after he was begging. Oxy was bullheaded and stubborn, so for him to beg was something big, and she knew that.

She fell to her knees and kissed Oxy softly on the lips.

"You have to promise me you won't ever cheat on me again, Brandon. You hurt me to the core. Just like you don't have a mother, I don't have one either anymore. Other than my friends, you were the closest thing to me," Amiah said with tears streaming down her face.

"I swear, I'll never fuck up again, but you have to promise to never shut a nigga out. If you're having an issue, communicate with me, babe. You know I am always listening."

Amiah continued to kiss him on his cheek and neck.

"I promise, baby. I am yours, forever. Now, can you propose to me the right way? Last night was so tacky."

Amiah shook her head and laughed in between sniffles. Oxy chuckled and stood up. He walked over to the table and picked up the ring. He gazed at it, thinking about when he first bought it. Now that she was back in his life, and his money was longer than it was when he first got it, he decided on going out to get her a new ring. Until then, he was going to propose with the one he had.

He walked back over to Amiah and smiled. He truly felt like she was worth the chase. She was his heartbeat, and his heart was broken without her. Seeing her with another dude, really made him realize he could be replaced. He knew Amiah didn't want for anything and could take care of herself. That's why he knew he had to win her back by showing her that he really loved her and not with gifts and money. He had beaten niggas up for her, killed everyone that caused problems in their relationship, and it was all worth it.

He got down on one knee. He looked up at Amiah with a serious look on his face. The way his life was moving, he needed her in it to stabilize him. He was ready to have children and be a family with her. He knew they both had a lot going on in their lives, but he knew they would be able to handle it all.

"You are the woman I want to grow old with, have my babies, and be by my side, no matter what. So, Amiah N'jae, will you be my wife?"

Oxy smiled.

"Yes, Brandon Lavell Merrier. I will marry you."

Oxy slid the ring on her finger and stood up. They knew it was going to take more time for them to heal their broken relationship, but they were both up for the challenge. The two of them stayed in Oxy's suite, loving on each other all day and enjoying each other's company. It had been so long since they had done that, and it felt good.

I'm Sorry

(Two months later...)

Amiah sat at the park with N'mere, Jr., watching him chew on his teething ring and make bubbles with his drool in his stroller. It was her day to watch him while Bayley and Meeze took their daughter to the doctor. Amiah loved spending time with N'mere, Jr., so she could get the feel of having a baby. She was now three weeks pregnant and ready to break the news to Oxy. She knew he was going to be happy, but she had something else for him that she knew would make him even happier.

A lot had happened when they were broken up, and she felt like some of it was her fault too, even though Oxy never blamed her for anything. The one thing she felt bad about was breaking up his mother's crystal. Oxy never mentioned he was upset about it, but she knew he didn't like bringing up his mother at all. She wanted to make up for her mistake and officially put everything in the past.

Amiah smiled when she spotted Oxy walking through the park with food from Panera Bread. He walked up to the table and sat the food down. Amiah stood up to hug him.

"What's up, babe? How are you and my nephew doing? I didn't know he was with you. I would have brought him a toy or something."

Amiah laughed and sat down.

"You know Bay and N'mere don't want us buying him anymore toys. She caught me giving him a sucker this morning, and she almost died."

Oxy chuckled while he shook N'mere Jr.'s little hand.

"Yeah, you know Bay don't fuck around with that candy shit. So, what's up with you, babe? What you want to talk to me about?" Oxy said, getting straight to why he was there. Amiah had called him and asked if he could meet her at the park for lunch and some conversation. She also told him she had something important to tell him.

Amiah started digging into the bag of food and pulled out her soup and Caesar salad. After she pulled out her food, she reached under the baby's stroller and pulled out a silver gift bag.

"I wanted you to come here, because I wanted to apologize for breaking your mother's things the night we broke up. I've been doing some thinking about my mistakes when we broke up, and that was one of them. I never should have done that, and I am sorry."

She slid the bag to Oxy.

"I told you, babe… I wanted to leave all that in the past. You didn't damage everything, and I've been forgave you for that."

"I know. Just open the bag though, dang."

She laughed. She was anxious for him to see what was inside. Oxy dug in the bag and pulled out something wrapped in white paper.

"Oh shit! It's my mom's crystal angel. How did you get this?" Oxy asked with a cheesy smile. That was the first time Amiah ever saw him smile so brightly.

"I met a woman at that business seminar we went to that makes custom crystal pieces, and she made everything I broke. Your mother didn't have anything to do with anything we had going on. She didn't deserve that, so I owe this to my mother-in-law. Now… dig deeper into the bag."

She smiled. Oxy took out the five pieces Amiah replaced, and then looked inside the bag. There was a folded piece of paper with his name on it. He pulled the paper out and unfolded it. Oxy rubbed his face and sat the paper down after he read it.

"Damn, babe… you're pregnant?"

Oxy gazed at Amiah while she smiled with tears in her eyes.

"Yes. We're having a baby."

Oxy stood up and walked over to her. He kissed her on the forehead and made her stand up.

"Damn, you made my day with all this good news. I was having a shitty ass day. That's why I love you, because I felt like I was gon' have to come out of retirement and blast a nigga today. Even these corporate niggas make a nigga wanna get violent."

Amiah kissed his lips.

"Don't worry about it, babe. Now, all you have to worry about is me and our baby. Let's go play with our god baby before he starts crying. You know he is a crybaby."

Oxy chuckled.

"Yeah, this lil' nigga is a crybaby. I'm sure our kid is going to be spoiled like him too."

"Yeah, I'm sure."

Oxy and Amiah walked over to the swing set with N'mere and pushed him in a swing.

EPILOGUE

He's Mine

Amiah walked through Kaiser Hospital looking flawless in an all-black Chanel business suit. She had just come from a proposal meeting, and she nailed it. She was finally getting her first body lotion line in stores, and she knew she was going to be bringing in some dough. She was already selling it online, and women of color loved it. Now that her meeting was over, she was ready to nip some shit in the bud with a certain someone.

Things were going great with her and Oxy… so good that she finally decided to move in with him but still keep her condo for when she was in the city or had a long day at school. With the both of them running successful businesses, they were able to afford it, on top of planning her dream wedding in Bora Bora after she had their first child.

However, Erica had been blowing up his phone with text messages, talking trash about Amiah in every text she sent. Erica was the reason they were on bad terms, and she was no longer going to tolerate her trying to manipulate Oxy to be with her. Amiah had read all the text messages that he didn't respond to, so she was going to settle the vendetta that Erica had with Oxy face to face and on her own. Oxy had told her to just leave the situation alone, but Amiah was done with side hoes, so she was going to start setting the record straight.

Amiah walked up to the nurse's station, got a visitor's pass with a fake name, and headed to Erica's room number. She had already called the hospital ahead of time to see if she was still there, and she was. When she walked into Erica's room, she spotted her lying in her bed, typing on her laptop. Amiah walked in and closed the door. When Erica heard the door close, she looked up and laid eyes on Amiah. It had been a long time since she had seen her, and she wanted to keep it that way, because she did not like Amiah. Ever since she was introduced to her, she envied her. Amiah had everything she wanted, and it made her jealous. That's why she didn't have a care in the world that she had ruined their relationship.

"What's up, Ms. Gomez? How are you feeling?" Amiah said as she sat in the chair next to Erica's bed. She took her shades off and stuffed them inside her oversized Giuseppe bag.

"What the fuck do you want, Amiah? Your nigga is the reason why I am laid up in here, so I don't want to see you."

Erica frowned.

"But, you want to see my nigga though. You need to stop texting him, Erica. He doesn't want you. Didn't you get the memo when he only let you suck his dick?"

Amiah smirked.

"Look, bitch, don't get cute, because you have him right now. He ain't gon' want you forever. There is going to be someone smarter than you, prettier than you, and can suck dick better than you, come take him right away from your ass. Watch... don't think you will be his main bitch forever," Erica shot back at her. She was angry that Amiah had come into her hospital room, trying to talk down on her. She felt like Amiah was no better than her.

"Just stop texting my man, bitch, or it's lights out for your trampy ass."

Amiah grabbed her bag and stood up.

"Bye, bitch, and tell your man that I am going to let the cops know he killed my ex, Emanuel, and those girls they found by the river. Have a nice life loving on your man in the clank," Erica shouted. Hearing Erica say she was going to snitch on Oxy made her angry. She turned around and dropped her bag on the floor.

"What did you say, bitch?" Amiah asked with an evil look on her face.

"You heard what the fuck I said, bitch. He killed them for you, and you still dissed him. You aren't a down ass bitch. You are a weak bitch."

Amiah stormed over to Erica's bed and pulled her pillows from under her head. Amiah put the pillows over Erica's face and pressed on her face, smothering her. There was no way Oxy was going to jail for something that Pricey and Lucky deserved. Oxy was in a good place and promised he was done with his past. He was done with robbing, done with killing, and done with his weakness, girls. They were putting everything behind them, and Erica was not going to live to mess it up.

Erica kicked her legs to try and escape from Amiah, but she was becoming weak. Her shoulder was still weak from the bullet she had in it, and her stomach was still healing. After holding the pillow over her face for at least three minutes, Erica's body went limp. Amiah took the pillow from her face and her eyes were wide opened. She had never killed anyone before, but she would do anything for Oxy's freedom. She loved him to death and would do anything for him. Amiah picked up her bag and left as quickly as she came. She rushed out of the hospital and hopped into the passenger seat of Reeka's black AMG Benz, where she waited out front for Amiah, and drove off.

THE END... MAYBE!

A NOTE TO MY READERS

Dear Readers,

I know you guys enjoyed this series, but this is the last installment, for now. I am going to take a breather and get my thoughts together for what I want to write next... I have some spin offs in the works and maybe a collab, but check out my older books on Amazon under my previous self-published pen name Robin Chanel! Stay tuned. Follow me on Instagram @brandbulliesrobin find me on Facebook https://www.facebook.com/BrandBulliesRobin. Make sure y'all flood me with feedback on my social media pages! I feed off of feedback.

Thanks!

Love all y'all! Please leave your review on Amazon or Goodreads, if Amazon doesn't let you!

Looking for a publishing home?

Royalty Publishing House, Where the Royals reside, is accepting submissions for writers in the urban fiction genre. If you're interested, submit the first 3-4 chapters with your synopsis to submissions@royaltypublishinghouse.com.

Check out our website for more information: www.royaltypublishinghouse.com.

Text ROYALTY to 42828 to join our mailing list!

To submit a manuscript for our review, email us at
submissions@royaltypublishinghouse.com

Text RPHCHRISTIAN to 22828 for our
CHRISTIAN ROMANCE novels!

Text RPHROMANCE to 22828 for our
INTERRACIAL ROMANCE novels!

Get LiT!

Download the LiTeReader app today and enjoy exclusive

content, free books, and more

Do You Like CELEBRITY GOSSIP?

Check Out QUEEN DYNASTY!
Visit Our Site: www.thequeendynasty.com

CPSIA information can be obtained
at www.ICGtesting.com
Printed in the USA
LVOW10s1615310317
529202LV00009B/688/P